The Moment Before

Suzy Vitello

DIVERSIONBOOKS

Diversion Books
A Division of Diversion Publishing Corp.
443 Park Avenue South, Suite 1004
New York, New York 10016
www.DiversionBooks.com

For more information, email info@diversionbooks.com

First Diversion Books edition January 2014.

Print ISBN: 978-1-62681-167-6
eBook ISBN: 978-1-62681-164-5

For Kirk, who continues to cheer the loudest.

one

Sabine's car sits in the driveway like a tombstone. Bird droppings cover half the windshield and if you were in Ms. Bowerman's art class, she'd tell you they were beautiful as a Kandinsky. All toothpasty, thick, yellowish-white—interesting, maybe, but not beautiful. Not even pretty. Every day this month on my way to the bus stop I've passed those splatters on that dead Volvo and I feel it crying for Sabine. Inside, where its cold engine gets colder every day, I imagine that the car is aching for the girl who's now ashes heaped in a piece of Asian crockery. If I were that car, I'd wonder what happened to the girl who used to blast music and rev the engine and peel out of the high school parking lot much too fast each day.

Dad almost put the car on Craigslist, but then he didn't. "Little Bird, you're old enough for your license," he said. "Maybe we should save the Volvo for you."

I don't want my dead sister's car, but I nodded. Best not to argue with Dad these days.

It's the daffodils and tulips time of year. The warm of spring, more than a hint in the air. More smiles on dog-walkers' faces. Kids out past dinner shooting their winter-flat basketballs into bent and rusty hoops up and down our street. On the way to the bus, when I pass neighbors, they do that shy smile thing. Then look away. Just seeing me, I know it makes them sad all over again. A month is beyond when "sorry for your loss" seems appropriate, but not enough time has passed for people to be all normal and happy around me. I'm supposed to be part of the Greenmeadow Art Show tonight. They're giving me the Lilith Cupworth prize for my charcoal drawing of a homeless guy and his dog. *The Portland Journal* will do a piece for the Life & Lifestyles section. Clap, clap. Good for you. Here's your five-hundred dollar scholarship. Sorry your sister's dead.

My leggings and Goodwill coat, my purple Keds, the front half of my hair dyed emerald and the henna tattoo around my wrist like a bracelet—that's the uniform they all know Brady Wilson by, the way I was different than my cheerleader sister. But it's all just a stupid costume. A couple more months and then junior year is over. Maybe I won't even go back in September.

I kick a crumpled PBR can someone tossed near a bush. In my head, there's the rhythm of Sabine's voice chanting just like she's still here, playing our childhood game, safety, danger, safety, danger, past the various lawns on my street. I hear the bus squeaking to a stop around the corner. I should run, but don't.

When I get to school it's the after-the-bell silence. The retired-cop-hall-monitor guy peeks at me over his bifocals. His eyebrows say *Really*? Sometimes I nod an acknowledgement that I'm pushing it, but today I don't even do that. I'm numb. Empty. When will I look forward to the next thing? When will I feel like myself again?

"Take a seat, Ms. Wilson," says the trig teacher when I creep into class.

On the board are *sin*, *cos*, *tan* and *pi*. The wiggly line graph. It always kills me when a teacher calls a girl *Mizz* instead of Miss. As if. I forgot my calculator again, so another period wasted.

Once I'm settled in my chair, next to me Trey Markham farts. Then he offers the *I just farted* grin. A girl behind him giggles. The teacher scribbles a function on the greenish board. Then, immediately, he turns on the overhead projector and pulls the screen down over what he just scratched onto the greenboard. "Who can tell me…" he starts. He mentions something called a *cosecant*. Trey squeaks out another one as if prompted by a word that sounds sort of bowelish.

"Mr. Markham," says the teacher. "This information will be covered on the SATs this Saturday. Maybe you'd like to go entertain yourself in private while the rest of your classmates learn what they need to in order to get into college."

There's some laughter and throat-clearing muffled into fists.

I open my notebook and begin sketching the teacher, whose name I can never remember because he just appeared one day a few months back, after Miss Lekoski bailed for no apparent reason. He's Mr. Nobody. Mr. Faceless Teacher. The Pale Blue Dot, like that shot of earth from space. Just another geeky math guy with visible underarm sweat stains and wrinkled Dockers. I hate trig. Except I like the wiggly graphs. Mr. Blue Dot takes shape on my college-ruled notebook paper. His comb-over, his wire-framed glasses, his growing belly, and half-untucked shirt. In his thought bubble there's a slice of pizza and a clock featuring the minutes until he can have it.

Triangles.

Trig.

Trapped.

The door opens and in he walks. The boy who killed my sister.

"Take a seat Mr. Christopher," says Blue Dot. "This is the third time this week."

Connor Christopher shuffles to the seat in back. Heads

turn. Checking out the level of red in his eyes, no doubt.

Fucking stoner.

I can feel him back there. Loser. I start chewing on a dark green strand of my hair, and try not to think about that day. The sound of two hundred and fifty people gasping all at once. Sabine's neck snapping the instant her chin hit the floor.

"Sohcahtoa," says Blue Dot wiggling his dried out dry-erase marker on the plastic sheeting under the overhead lamp. "That's the shortcut, people. Soh. Cah. Toa."

There is whispering and texting going on behind me. Up on the wall above the board the clock says first period is half over. Trey Markham has his forehead on his folded arms now, feigning sleep. Cathi Serge, in the second row, has raised her hand. Right outside the open window, the *beep, beep, beep* of the school lunch delivery truck backing out of the bay accompanies Cathi's, "The tangent is the side opposite divided by the adjacent side."

Blue Dot points to the tip of his nose with the finger of one hand, and then levels the index finger of his other hand at Cathi. I can't see Cathi's face, but I know it's got a smug expression on it.

I was signed up for the SATs this Saturday, and since Sabine, well, everything's on hold.

There's a tug at the hem of my Goodwill coat. It's Martha Hornbuckle, on the side opposite Trey Markham. She points to her phone. Mine's out of batteries, so whatever she's texted me is swimming around invisibly, looking for a place to land. Like Sabine's soul. According to my grandparents, if we didn't attend mass and pray for her cremains, she would be forever in limbo. Data without a plan.

I gesture the *sorry* shrug, and turn my hand into an invisible writing implement. Martha scribbles something on a gas receipt and hands it to me across the skinny aisle. In

Martha's hasty penmanship, I can barely make out the words amid the $4 per gallon stamp from Chevron. *Norm's Chinese*, I think it says. *Lunch?* I scribble, *Can't* under it and hand it across to her. Immediately the little slip is tucked back into the top of my Ked. I see an inky question mark.

Setting up the art show, I write back, though it can hardly fit on the tiny slip, and before I have a chance to stretch my arm across the aisle again, Blue Dot swoops in and intercepts. Rebound for the math teacher. Everybody cheer.

"Ms. Wilson," he blusters. "The office."

That same finger he just used to let Cathi know she was *bingo, bingo, bingo, ding, ding, ding,* is now pointing beyond the fireproof door of math class. I've been dismissed. I'm in trouble. Bad, bad Brady.

I think about knocking over the desk chair as I stomp off, but, in that split second of being outside myself, watching myself behave badly, I choose the higher ground. I actually hear myself say, "Sorry," and I push my chair in, gather my stuff, and realize that Blue Dot did indeed have a chance to witness his unflattering likeness on my paper, so I say it again. "Sorry." With eye contact, even. That's when I hear Sabine's voice, clear as can be, saying *Atta girl, Midget.*

The management at Greenmeadow High is as burnt out as it gets. A principal who's a year from retirement. Then there's the vice principal who hides in his office unless the Portland Police requires him to fill out the odd minor-in-possession form. And forget about the guidance counselors. Statewide budget cuts mean we share two part-timers with the other west side high school. Because my sister died in the gymnasium, and my parents haven't decided whether to sue yet or not, nobody likes it when I'm sent here for insubordination. It makes the administrators squeamish. The secretary smiles, her chapped fleshy lips in need of balm. She points to the wooden bench. She'll buzz the vice principal, and he'll come out, his hand extended. I know the drill.

I chew a section of hair while I wait. Look at my stick-legs stretched out in front of me. The man's trench coat I'm wearing. This coat, in its former life, it could have been one worn by a pervert. One of those guys who sneaks into darkened movie theaters, sidles up next to teenage girls, and plays with himself. Gross. Truthfully, I'm a little over the lame art-girl costume myself. Tired of looking like the rebellious little sister. I'm nobody's little sister anymore.

Really, if I'm honest, who I want to be is Martha. Everyone likes Martha. She's a shoe-in for this year's Greenmeadow Rose Festival Princess. She organizes coat drives, blood drives, do-not-drives. Last spring she brought a shovel to school, and before classes, out there in the rain, she tilled the community garden bed, making it ready for the seniors to plant their peas. Swear. Once, she gave a pity hand job to Walter Pine, the Lego Robotics wiz, and when he spread it around she told everyone that he had a really big dick. That's how kind she is. Straight A's. Athletic enough for Varsity basketball. Smart enough for the debate team. Cool enough to be my friend. At least that's what she tells me. And when Sabine died? She did everything right. She came by and cleaned her room, found the best photo for the obit. Organized casseroles. We still have six pans of lasagna in the freezer. Thanks to Martha.

Martha, Sabine and I go way back. In grade school, before she became super-perfect, Martha and I hung out all the time. In middle school though, things changed. Martha hungered for all that stuff that goes along with being chosen. She wanted the starring role in every play. Solo performances in choir. Fastest mile in gym class. There was only one girl who beat her out of things, and that was my sister. Martha studied Sabine. Copied her. Cozied up to her. While I drifted off into my own world. Sketching, painting, daydreaming with brush and pencil. Once we got to Greenmeadow, Martha changed again. Became the Queen of Community Service. Maybe that's why she started hanging out with me. Some sort of charity work.

"You're lucky," Martha told me once. "You don't care what other people think. You're so good at being you."

I'm not feeling so lucky today, is what I'm thinking when the vice principal, Mr. Call-me-Leonard Field, smiles and thrusts his hand out to me. "How are you, Brady?"

"Here, so, probably not great?"

"You're in the running for the Cupworth tonight, right?"

I shrug, but conjure my Inner Martha just in time to offer a polite, humble head cock, to which Field invites a fist bump.

My knuckles meet his knuckles.

He makes the come-to-my-office gesture then leads the way, directing me to a comfy, Naugahyde bad student chair to slump down in.

The office door clicks shut behind me and "Leonard" winds around to behind his desk, sits, and then starts right in. "Having some trouble in math, eh?"

Leonard Field's much-younger wife and their two toddler boys glare at me from his messy desk. Odd that his family wouldn't be facing him.

"Not my favorite subject I guess."

"You know, I had a hard time with trig." Leonard tick-tocks his head as though conjuring up his long-ago days. "Nearly flunked it."

Martha, what she would do now is she'd nod, lock eyes with the vice principal. She might offer, *I really have to put in more time. Maybe a tutor?* She might ask, *So, how did you end up succeeding?* If she were really on her game, she might compliment the holiday sweaters on Leonard's kids—or remark on his wife's stunning good looks. Martha will either be the next Mother Teresa or the head of PR for Viagra. I say, "Is it too late to drop it?"

Leonard Field takes a sip from a stained mug, and sets it on a stack of papers. He leans back in his old-fashioned wooden office chair and the springs squeak. His hands clasp behind his head. "Brady. How are you? I mean, really, how *are* you?"

For a second I contemplate that he's sincere. Maybe he *does* care about this grieving-squarepeg-girl. How would I respond in a matchingly sincere way? And then I think what if I had died and Sabine was sitting here in my place? Her mascara trails would be black bars on her face. Her UPC code cheeks, her red eyes. Girl tears. The sort of wailing grief that comforts a man like Leonard Field. "I guess I'm looking forward to tonight. The art show and the prize," I lie, and then force the ends of my lips up into my cheeks.

"That's my girl," says the vice principal of the highest test-scoring high school in Oregon.

I meant it half as a joke, but it's stunning how a little white lie has that sort of power. I can almost see him crossing off *fix Brady* from his to-do list. The conversation with Trophy Wife, later, over dinner, while the hellions throw SpaghettiOs at each other: *The Wilson girl, she had a breakthrough in my office today. All it takes, sometimes, is someone to listen.*

He leans forward, piercing eye contact. "Is it hard, Brady, to have Connor in your classes?"

He's in two of them. "No. Well, yes. Sometimes."

"I've been wondering if we should intervene," he says. "You know?"

Not even Martha will give Connor the time of day. "Whatever," I say, and then, because I know that that word will undo the whole breakthrough hope, I quickly add, "you think is best."

two

Irish twins are siblings born within a year of each other. Sabine was born in September; I came along the following August. We started kindergarten the same year. Me: sucking my thumb, wetting my pants, not knowing the alphabet. Her: already reading, bossing the boys around, teacher's pet. Free day care, my mom joked, delighted that I made the cut-off, by days, so she could get her realtor's license and start selling high-end homes.

Nobody would have mistaken us for real twins.

Sabine's big blue eyes and reddish-blond hair, she took after Dad's side. The Scottish Wilsons, robust in every way. Storytellers, sports-minded, excellent at business. Sabine was a chip-off-the-old-jock—a true daughter of John Wilson, the ex-minor-league pitcher with a major-league heart. Prone to tantrums and public displays of affection.

In third grade, for Halloween, Sabine dressed up as Marge Simpson, and she made the boy she referred to as her *boyfriend* dress up as Homer. She practiced the voice, and had a different skit worked out with every stop on their trick-or-treat tour. The poor little Homer boyfriend couldn't keep up. He handed his pillowcase and the few fun-sized candies to Sabine after the fifth house. A trick-or-treater tendering his resignation, just like that, in the face of such pressure. She wore you out, if you were her friend. There was always some next thing bubbling up in her head.

Suzy Vitello

Mom called her *my manic-panic girl*. Me? *Brady-brooder*.

I take after the Italian Panapentos. Dark, Sicilian, Catholic. Mom's side of the family, they keep their cards close to the chest. Olive-skinned, raven-eyed, surly and superstitious. My Nona paints in heavy oils. Still lifes. A bowl of peaches in the foreground, and if you look real close, there's a skull behind the table, looming on a shelf. A Where's Waldo sort of hidden death object. My grandparents are the type of Catholics who still eat fish every Friday. There's a dead Jesus and last year's palm frond nailed above their pushed together twin beds.

In case you're wondering, I was left back that kindergarten year, after my eye started twitching.

Don't get me wrong. I loved my sister. I never, not once, wished her dead.

After I leave Leonard Field's office, heading to art, crunching scraps of crepe paper ribbon left over from a locker that was recently "birthdayed," it hits me. The entire building, the whole culture of this enormous suburban public high school, deflated when Sabine died. I'm not making this up. Her energy was so strong, the lunch ladies named a dish for her. Sa-beans. It was after the cheering squad won state last year, my sister as Captain. The lunch ladies dyed the refried beans Greenmeadow green in her honor. They strung a banner across the hot food line—a poster-sized photo of Sabine doing her winning high-splits pyramid stunt. It sounds almost pornographic; the idea of students lining up under her crotch for their burritos, but, my sister transcended that sort of typecasting. You got the feeling, looking at the stretched out cheerleader grin on her face, that she could lift the entire football team over the goalpost with that smile.

Her boyfriend, Nick Avery, he all but dropped out after

the accident. Class president, captain of the lacrosse team, the only guy in the whole school who could have possibly had a chance with my sister. They were beyond King and Queen of Prom. So beyond Class Couple. They had a Facebook page called *Beenick* with, like, over 1200 followers. High school paparazzi tagging Brangelina-esque pictures to their wall. Now, a sort of boyfriend widower, he wears black clothes Johnny Cash style, his squinty eyes covered by Versaces. His locker, which I pass now, is still decorated with the plastic flowers of a gypsy grave. As if she died here while in the middle of a kiss, there's a snapshot of them making out, toddler alphabet magnets spelling RIP holding the photo in place.

The overhead fluorescent panels twitch. I hear the shushing of my coat against my legs and then the echoes of that shush. Greenmeadow is shaped like a capital E. A long hallway and three arms. Two stories of that. Art is in a modular trailer outside, and in order to get to it between classes, you have to go way down the last arm of the E, then out the only open door, where the ex-cop usually stands to make sure nobody is cutting class, or no disturbed, revenge-seeking shooters are trying to sneak in. Today, he's not at his station; the door is ajar and unguarded.

I realize I could easily skip, and nobody would be the wiser. For all Ms. Bowerman knows, I'm still in Field's office. I could, if I wanted, slip out the door, and down to Starbucks. Or, I could go back home. Or, I could hop the bus and go to the zoo. It's a gorgeous day. One of those surprisingly warm early spring days that makes you feel like you cheated the calendar. The sky a sea of solid blue. If I walked up to the water tower, winding above Greenmeadow, I would see the white upside-down sugar cone that is Mt. Hood. Maybe I should skip the rest of school, the assembly, tonight's art show and go—where?

An angle of sun slices into my face when I push open the door and step outside. For a second it seems like that blinding light at the end of the tunnel near-death-experience people speak of. And then, the weird thing that's been happening lately, the sense that Sabine is hovering over me like a spy plane. Watching me. Judging me. *Go to class Brady. Don't be such a little fuckup.* The modular art building sits off to my right, the edge of campus to the left.

Sabine: *Art.*

Me: *Freedom.*

Sabine: *You owe this to me; to them.*

Me: *I owe nothing; you're the one who bailed.*

Sabine: *I'd trade places with you in a heartbeat.*

Me: *Fine. Let's rewind the clock and I'll take a header to the gym floor and you can wander around this hellhole instead.*

Sabine: *That's so unfair.*

Me: *Nobody said death was fair.*

I'm walking, walking, walking away from the direction I should walk if I'm going to art, having this insane conversation, hearing my sister like she's right next to me, my eyes focused down at the purple of my sneakers, and a shadow cuts my path. The long blade of a shadow.

"Shit," I hear being murmured from between two cars in the student parking lot.

Keep walking, says Sabine. *Don't look over there.*

I would keep walking if I had truly committed to skipping out on the Cupworth and the let's-pretend-art's-important assembly. But I'm still in limbo with it all. A text message looking for a turned on phone. The *shit*, the voice of it, is older than a high school student mixed with too young for the real world. It's Connor Christopher smoking a bowl, crouched between the cars like he's in Afghanistan surveying land mines. Even in his bent-over posture, he can't disguise those long legs, that broad chest. Gym-worked arms half-covered in a button-down shirt rolled up at the sleeves. He's baked.

Down the parking lot, coming out of a pickup truck with a Venti-sized Starbucks in his hand, is that geezer-cop-turned-high-school nark. I have two choices: stay where I am, out in the open and get popped by his mortar round, or duck down quick, crouch down next to Connor, in the trenches. *Face the music*, says Sabine.

I crouch. Half-crawl between the cars, one finger to my lips. "Garrison," I mouth. Connor nods. We're on the same team, all of the sudden. Comrades in the war against the war against drugs.

Connor tucks his pipe into his pocket. Slip-slides his butt to the asphalt, lets out a sigh. He's not looking at me.

The skunky weed smell in the air between us. Lots of other stuff in the air between us. I'm counting to a hundred in my head, thinking that the coast will be clear by then, and I can pop back up. Shuffle my ass to art after all. *Good plan*, counsels my dead sister.

I'm at seventy-eight in my head, and Connor says, "Just so you know, I wasn't stoned that day."

My head jerks around all *Exorcist* and I take in his man-sized frame. His sandy-blond hair and green eyes. I could draw him, this boy, and .nake him a god. I'm getting a prize for a sketch I did of a man a quarter the specimen. This healthy, OK, gorgeous, perfectly proportioned chunk of boy. Out of my mouth comes, "Fuck. Off."

Then, I stand up like there're springs in my knees, brush the gravelly bits from my trench coat and leggings, and, without looking back at the loser, I stride off to class.

three

Mom is breathtakingly fragile in her couture costume. At forty-five she can still pull off a Betsey Johnson and not look like a total cougar. Since Sabine died, she's gotten even more beautiful. A sort of widow look reminiscent of photos I've seen of First Lady Jackie Kennedy. Oversized sunglasses, the occasional silk headscarf. Grieving chic, that Sonia Panapento Wilson. And Dad? He looks like shit. He barely tucks in his shirts anymore. Stains on his clothes, a half-shaven face. His last haircut was for the memorial service. Mom tells him he needs to pull it together for tonight. She's saying this from the guest bathroom while spritzing product into her hair.

"Don't start, Sonia," he mutters. He's pawing through the collection of sports jackets in the hall closet, and he finally selects one, clears his throat, and sighs. Then there's the sound of hangers falling off the rod. He's become clumsy; he's probably drunk. From the living room chair, where I'm still snuggled under Nona's black and gray afghan, I call out, "You don't have to go, you know."

Dad whips around, his jacket hanging loosely on his diminished frame, a couple of choices of tie in his hands. "Brady, I wouldn't miss this for the world."

It's their first public appearance since Sabine's memorial. I can smell the whiskey on Dad's breath all the way in the next room. The dark circles under his eyes, his greasy cowlick, people will wonder if he was the model for my prize-winning charcoal of the homeless guy. I wish the two of us could just stay home. Nap under this warm blanket and let gorgeous Mom accept the prize on my behalf. Didn't some movie star do that once at the Oscars?

"Are you dressed yet, Brady?" calls the movie star in our house, who just happens to also be a first-gen Italian Princess.

Sigh.

"Brady, you better get a move on," chimes Dad, examining the face of his watch under his cuff.

The fuzzy afghan is my shawl as I shuffle to my room. Everything's a mess. On my bed are the choices: the same leggings I wore earlier with a sixties house dress meant for someone with twenty pounds more boob, a faux-Victorian gown, all lace and shimmer and high neck. Neither of these options feels right. They expect me to dress all weirdly artsy, of course. I have to look the part. A pair of black skinny jeans with an electric blue sweater dress. An Oregon Trail pioneer apron over Pleather pants. Converse sneakers, boys' boxers, a unitard. The trench coat lies in a heap of outwear against my dresser. Ski pants? Maybe a tutu under a hand-knit car coat? Feeling shivery, I pull the Nona blanket tighter around me.

"We're leaving in ten," calls Mom.

My cell is charging on my desk and it's beeping every three seconds with texts. Well-wishers. Frenemies. BFFs. When I scroll down the list, it's mostly Martha. Dear Martha. She wants to sit next to me tonight, hold my hand. I don't read through them, but I feel her boosting spirit. I see the X's and O's that fill the screen. If love flies through the air but the recipient isn't actually paying attention, does it count?

Want to wear one of my dresses?

It takes me a minute to understand what's going on with that offer. More than a minute, actually, for the idea to penetrate.

The red Juicy with the back zip; you'd look stunning in that.

The thought of the trespass. Actually crossing that threshold. Butterflies hatch and flutter in my gut. I've only set foot in Sabine's room once since her death.

The one I wore to Freshman Fling. I think it'd be the perfect fit.

The happiness in her voice. That same voice that led her tribe to cheering victory.

The black shawl and I creep out of my room minutes before the honk of the horn will announce takeoff. Under the shawl, I slink along in my slippers, and now I'm in front of her room. My hand on the brass knob, the click and whoosh of the door against carpet. The faint smell of Dolce & Gabbana perfume.

Inside, it's like when Dorothy leaves black-and-white Kansas and enters Technicolor Oz. I want to freeze the moment and take it all in. Evening light bathes Sabine's perfectly made bed and brightens up another Nona creation—a quilt, in various shades of rose. Three sets of pillows are stacked neatly, emerging from the headboard. An American Girl cheerleader doll rests against the center pillow, grassy-green pom-poms wedged into its tiny plastic hands.

How can I even touch this? My sister's life.

On her dresser, a collection of five-by-sevens. Sabine and I, little girls in matching Easter dresses. The Greenmeadow cheerleaders in a pile, Sabine doing her famous splits down in front. The junior year winter formal shot—Nick and Sabine all fancied up, about to board the rented limo. She still had braces back then, so her smile is closed-lipped, but just as big as always, it spreads to the edges of her face. Nick's hair is gelled into ridges, like someone took a wide-tooth comb through wet cement. His head is shaped like an urn. I've never understood why everyone thinks he's hot.

In front of the five-by-sevens there's a smaller photo of

Sabine, Martha and I at our beach house one long-ago summer. Martha is French-braiding one side of my hair and Sabine is doing the other. There's a caption on the photo in one of those Photoshoppy scripts, and it reads: *The Annual Brady Braiding Contest.* Funny, I'd forgotten all about that, the way Sabine and Martha would make anything into a competition, and most of the time, there I was, caught in the middle.

Sabine's iPhone lays there, a paperweight on top of bereavement cards my parents still can't bear to read. Her greeting, *This is Sabine. Give me a "G" and have a great day.* No promise of getting back to the caller. No instructions. Just an order. You *must* have a great day. I listen to her tell me that at least once every day. The sound of her voice making the blood from my heart mix with the blood in my belly. Not butterflies, exactly. Maybe moths.

"Brady." from Mom, clackity-clacking against the slate floor foyer.

Thanks to Martha Hornbuckle and her post-mortem helper-bee activities, Sabine's closet is color-coded. The scarlet dress she wants me to wear tonight is grouped with a bunch of fiery frocks. Everything from pale red to the deep purple of a fresh bruise. It's there in the middle, encased in dry-cleaning plastic, this $300 dress she wore only once. I peel off the shawl, my sweats. I'm almost naked now, in my dead sister's bedroom.

I look down at my flat chest. At the Freshman Fling dress. My boobs are ping pong balls. There's no way.

Maybe there's something in Sabine's underwear drawer. Do I dare to? Closing my eyes, holding my breath, I yank open Sabine's top dresser drawer. Her Victoria's Secret lingerie. Piles of pink panties. My hand grazes the silky underthings, sifts through them, and then lands on one of her outgrown Wonderbras. The add-a-size pushup type. I adjust the straps— the fancy ribbon woven through it reminds me of the hair ribbons woven into our braids in that photograph of us. After I fasten the hooks, looking Sabine's full-length mirror I don't even recognize my boobs. Voila, magic, I've got a mini rack. It's like someone airbrushed them on.

The front door opens and closes. In thirty seconds, I'll hear the Ford Fusion purring in the driveway. Quickly, off goes the dry cleaning bag and on goes the dress. There in the mirror, reflected back, is someone I don't recognize.

Sabine says, *Holy cow, Midget.*

Yep. Not bad. But the green hair, the heavy eyeliner, I need to soften my look. Again I pillage Sabine's storehouse of girl things. Eye makeup remover, Maybelline Volum' Express, some foundation to cover a zit. Lip gloss.

I spray a whiff of Dolce & Gabbana and slap at the air. Just the smell of her. It's almost too much. The horn honks.

I grab Sabine's hairbrush, slip on a pair of her platform sandals—which are the only thing of Sabine's a bit too small for me—and with a fistful of my sister's cosmetics, I'm out the door.

In the car, Dad and Mom are tense. They don't look up or sideways when I scurry into the backseat; they don't have a clue what I'm wearing. I could still be in my sweats for all they know. Lately, when they're in the same place, my parents go robot. Their bodies get paralyzed around each other, eyes looking to the next thing. Dad mechanically swivels his head as we reverse. Sabine's sad Volvo watches us back out the drive.

Mom says, "Are you OK to drive?"

The smell of whiskey. The smell of perfume. The smell of tension.

Dad says, "I'm fine."

Mom says, "How long will this presentation go, do you think?"

Tonight's ceremony is a fundraiser. Our art will be on

display with price tags and little red stickers when a piece gets sold, just like in an actual gallery. Only, it isn't a gallery. It's the long spine of the "E" with balsawood and canvas screens set up to hide the lockers. Fake walls for the student art. Ms. Bowerman expects my homeless guy will fetch enough money for new sable brushes.

Like Mom, I wish the whole thing could be over lickety-split, but hearing her impatience, it feels like an ice cube shoved down my Wonderbra. My heart shrinks from the coldness.

"Few hours, tops," I say, meanly.

"Have a hot date or something," chuckles Dad, conjuring some of that ex-jock cockiness he's usually known for.

Mom gives him the stinkeye, which I can see in the rearview.

"You can just drop me off," I say. "No biggie."

"Oh, Brady, Sweetie," says Mom, lurching her gaze toward me, "I'm so pr— what the hell? Is that Sabine's dress?"

The gloss wand between my thumb and fingers, gliding across my bottom lip, turns into a poison pen. Mom's eyes go pinprick and she lasers me up, down, noting all my sister's items in my hand, on my lap.

"Yeah," I tell her. "It is."

"What in the world?" Mom says.

Dad's eyes are on the road, then in the rearview, on the road again. I see his corneas go glassy in the mirror.

"I think she wants me to wear it," I murmur.

Mom clears some phlegm from her throat. "You should have asked."

"Asked? Who? You?"

"Your father and I…" she starts, then switches gears. "It is inappropriate, Brady."

I slide the gloss applicator back into its tube and look down at my newly formed cleavage, and mutter, "But, somehow it's fine for you to dress like her."

"That's enough, Little Bird," chimes Dad.

Robots united.

"If we weren't already running late, I'd have us turn back, so you could change into your own clothes." Mom is shaking. The hair on her arms lifted up all static electricity-ish.

Don't cry, Midge. Hang tough.

"I just don't know what you were thinking is all. How many of Sabine's things have you swooped in and grabbed? Like some v…"

Mom cut herself off before saying *vulture.*

"Sonia, let it go," whisper-talks Dad. "This is Brady's night."

"It's just so…insensitive."

Dad changes the subject. "I was thinking we might go the beach house for this weekend. You know, for Easter? Get away from rainy old Portland?"

Given that the day has been record-breaking lovely for mid-April, I find this statement funny. But not quite funny ha-ha. "The beach, yeah. That would be good."

"There's no way I can get away now. I've got three listings. An open house coming up."

"Sonia. It's Easter for Chrissake. I think we need to get away as a family."

Clearly, Dad's been thinking about this for a while.

"So, tonight is spring-all-sorts-of-things-on-Sonia night, eh? What next, John, you want to adopt a Chinese baby?"

My mother's cruel asides are famous for the way they bump up against comical. Her tongue is quick—something she passed down to me. Our therapist says that's at the heart of our trouble with each other. We're too alike.

Dad pulls into the Greenmeadow parking lot, and we come to a stop near a patch of lawn adjoining the football stadium, a big G of freshly planted marigolds glows at us as we exit the car. It's as warm as summer out, but breezy, and Sabine's dress blows up a little, the hem grazing my thighs. The tickle of this feels like a secret I'm sharing with my sister, like back when we were little girls sneaking into each other's rooms at night to munch on candy under the blankets.

Our school, which sits two miles east of the Portland boundary with high-tech Washington County, is known for those things every school wants to be known for: top test scores, winning sports teams and low dropout numbers. It's also known as the school that had two suicides and an accidental death this year. Greenmeadow is ripe for one of those *60 Minutes* exposés where they uncover all the student stress and drug use. If my parents go forward with a lawsuit, it'll take more than a Thursday night art auction to refill the Tupperware containers with studio clay.

Mom is preoccupied with the little rectangle of a phone in her hand. I can't help it, but she's driving me crazy, so I say, "Mom, will you just relax?"

She stops in her tracks, yoga-breathes a sigh out her nose. Dad and me and her, our diminished family in a cluster on the walkway, people have to step around us as we stand still and gaze at the weeping cherry blossoms on a nearby tree. "This isn't easy for us, Little Bird," says Dad, still focused on the tender, graceful branches. "We know how important, how huge, really, this honor is. Our daughter, the artist."

"Thanks," I manage, in robot-tone.

The building in front of us, it's like going to a wrecking yard and witnessing the scrap metal of a fatal car crash. They were there, in the bleachers. One second their oldest daughter was twirling on the tops of fingertips, and the next, down on the polished gym floor, her skin the only thing holding her head on. Ribbons of red ooze out her ear, her nose, her mouth.

I was there, too. Hanging out with Desiree and Joni and

Madison, all of us in a cluster at the far end of the bleachers—mad, because there's this pressure to join in with rah-rah school spirit. We sat there, the group of us, sketching, journaling, doodling. Our pink and electric blue and emerald green hair. Our henna tattoos. Resentful, eye-rolling. Nobody knew what was about to happen. Especially me.

When Sabine hit the floor instead of her partner's basket-catching arms, I was sketching a pair of little girls sitting in the bleachers on the other side of the gym. They had these huge matching bows in their hair—sisters, probably. Aspiring cheerleaders. They were so cute, the girls. It wasn't until their hands covered their mouths in one quick flash, and my ears took in the sound of two hundred fifty people in the gymnasium gasping together, that I realized something was wrong.

Now, in the fading afternoon light, Mom reaches into her bag for her sunglasses. The tiniest of wrinkles around her top lip gather and deepen as she tightens her jaw. I'm not sure what they want me to say. Should I apologize further? Should I comfort them? Sabine died a couple days before spring break, and once school started up again, there I was, back in class. I've darkened the doors of this crypt every day for the past three weeks. My parents aren't ready. I can still smell whiskey on my father's breath. This was an enormous mistake, coming here. It's too soon.

When we reach the upper lot, there, as expected, is my grandparent's Lincoln. Both front doors are ajar; the skinny, crippled limbs of my Nona and Nono emerging like the legs of a lunar vehicle. "Here we go," mutters Mom under her breath.

The unspoken assignment distribution. I get Nona, Mom gets Nono, and my dad, the Protestant heathen, can damn well keep his hands to himself. My Nona's purse weighs more than she does, and I slip it around my arm as I help her out of the car. "Thanks so much for coming, Nona," I say as my four-foot-ten grandmother grunts to a stand.

As always, she presses her wrinkled hand against the flesh of my cheek, maneuvers my face so I'm looking down at her black eyes, her deep, red painted cheeks. Her penciled-in brows and the ever-growing mole on the side of her bulbous nose. "Mia *nipote*," she says through tightly pursed crimson lips. "How beautiful you look tonight. Papi, doesn't our girl look good?"

Shuffling around the back bumper of the car, Nono holds up and waves his cane in greeting. Mom trails behind, still glancing at her phone every few seconds.

Dad waits near the entrance of the school, his arms folded. He's lost so much weight this month; he looks like he's wearing borrowed clothes. He holds the door for us as we trudge on in under the brightly painted Art Night banner. My feet are beginning to ache in Sabine's too-small sandals. I look up. The throngs of people we were supposed to be navigating the grandparents around are not here. A dozen arts-supporter type parents, mostly volunteers, mill about the hall. A mom hands out programs, which are really just advertisements for donations, with the scissor mark line and who-to-make-the-check-out-to language.

Everyone is smiling as we pass. We're the red carpet party at this affair. The family of the dead girl, plus, guess what, the family of the scholarship recipient. Does anybody smell a rat?

My homeless guy and his dog sit on an easel just outside the entrance to the *cafetorium*. Nona stops me. "You work." she marvels. "Oh, *Nipote*. This is good stuff. Papi, look at Brady's art."

"It really is, Bird," says Dad. "You take after Granny."

Nona tenses on my arm. She hates that *Granny* business. But she settles right down, and pats me on the hand. "I am so proud."

After we get everyone installed in their seats I hear the tell-tale voice of Martha enter the venue. Of course, she's being helpful. Ushering the last minute stragglers to various chairs in front. Greenmeadow has a real auditorium, but the Art Awards Night didn't rank high enough to get to use it. Plus, there's a leak in the roof over the stage that isn't fixed yet, and you can't be too careful with scheduling an event in the rainy months. Which is every month, basically.

There is the chit-chat of neighbors checking in with each other, a few cells phones clicking off. Martha slides into the seat next to me that I saved for her, and pinches my upper arm, "Nice dress."

"It's Sabine's," I whisper. "And the family's a little upset I'm wearing it."

At the cue *family*, Martha, ever the mannerly one, extends her hand to Nona on my opposite side, "Mrs. Panapento, so good to see you again." Then she waves at the rest of the crew, who are dribbled out in the adjoining seats.

"You didn't answer my text, Brady. Can you go out after? I really want to catch up. I have something to tell you."

"I don't know," I whisper. "It's a school night and all."

The lights flicker, a little Pavlovian thing for the youngsters to quiet us all down. The audience fumbles their hands to pockets and purses; the very last of the cell phones get shut off. A dying murmur spreads throughout the *cafetorium*. Mom glances one more time at her device, and then slips it into her purse. Nona pinches my arm.

The principal strides onstage and rambles about the importance of art—though, everyone here knows he's ready to scrap it in favor of another AP Chemistry class. He introduces Bowerman, who, I have to say, does her best to hide her open hostility toward the admin suits. She's in rare form, what with her dreads and parachute pants and super loud, deep voice. "In our struggle to understand the complexities of our times, art matters more than ever," she says to the sound of polite applause.

Ms. Bowerman really is terrific, and sincere. She's that cool teacher who'll stick her neck out for students, write long, detailed letters of recommendation to colleges. She'll stand toe-to-toe against the committees that favor teach-to-the-test over creative inquiry. Words like *creative inquiry*, and *public discourse*, and *cultural innovators* fill the hall. Nona's Chiclet breath moves in, "Why is she wearing those weird pants?"

"Nona," I whisper back. "Behave yourself."

Ms. Bowerman finishes off her speech with, "Now, let's give a warm welcome to our favorite patron, Mrs. Lilith Cupworth."

Applause.

Mrs. Cupworth takes the stage. She's perfectly coiffed. All lilacs and tweed. She positions the microphone toward her lips, then doesn't say anything at all, just stares out at the chairs. The silence gets awkward. Finally, out her mouth comes, "I'm disappointed."

A few throats clear.

"By my count, there are fifty, maybe sixty at this event."

More silence, and Mrs. Cupworth slowly swivels her head from one side of the *cafetorium* to other. I glance at the principal who has taken a step toward the podium. Does he plan on pulling her off the stage?

"If this were a pep rally," she offers, emphasizing the *p* at the end of *pep*, "for a football game. It would be standing room only."

It's like this woman is channeling me. Finally, someone not smothered in bullshit. I look at Martha, whose eyes are bulging.

"If we continue to treat art as some sort of side sauce," says Mrs. Cupworth, "I'm afraid we will soon have a society made up merely of Philistines and dullards."

I glance down at my pushed up boobs, my fancy red lap.

"The cheap thrill. The ball through the goal posts. The titillation of bosoms on the Internet. These are easy ways to fleeting, surface reaction. Art does not come cheaply, ladies and gentlemen. One must nurture the soul in order to grow one's appreciation for beauty. For aesthetic. If we care more about sport than the very foundation of humanity, we are doomed."

The principal licks his lips, nervously.

What's with the disrespecting of sports, Sabine wants to know.

Or maybe it's Martha who says that.

I can't, now, take my eyes off of this Mrs. Cupworth. I watch her manhandle the microphone, her elderly fingers caressing it, bending it, letting it go, and then she pivots, one hand on the stem of the mic, the other, *j'accuse*, directed at our fearless leader. She barks, "Every year you chop, chop, chop. When will it end? We have but one substantive visual art class in the curriculum, and with the others, you've bastardized the content to blend in technology studies and, God help me, P.E."

It's true. We have a class called *dynamic arts*, where you take a sketchpad and walk up to the water tower. If it's decent weather, you draw up there. If it's raining, you take pictures with your phone, then download the images in computer lab and manipulate them in Photoshop.

You could hear a Bobby pin drop. Everyone is holding their breath. The principal's face is the color of virgin canvas. Ms. Bowerman, on the other side of the stage, is doing something with a dreadlock. Is she chewing it? And still, Ms. Cupworth's finger wags. "Take a stand. As the administrator of this bastion of secondary education, you have an obligation to do so."

Now he walks swiftly up to the podium, clapping his

hands as cue that applause is called for because this speech is over. The audience obeys. Nona, next to me, proceeds to lurch out of her chair and I join her. We will give Mrs. Lilith Cupworth a standing ovation, why not?

The principal reaches the mic and says, "Quite an inspired and passionate speech from our dear benefactor. What do you say, ladies and gentlemen? Let's give it up for Mrs. Cupworth and proceed to honor our art students with this year's awards."

There is sweat on his forehead. I can see the beads of it under the lights. Ms. Bowerman joins them at the podium once again, and reveals a stack of manila envelopes. Nobody but Nona and I are standing, so we stop clapping and sit back down. Martha squeezes my hand. I feel like I'm at the Oscars, when they scan all the faces of the nominees and you try not to look disappointed when you don't win. Bowerman told me I'm getting it, but, with the craziness of tonight, anything could happen.

There are honorable mentions. Third and second prizes, which are gift certificates to Blick. It is announced that Dobson Caruthers and Brittany Hasslebrock get those. Mrs. Cupworth, back to being sweet and ladylike, hands the envelopes to them as they trot on stage. She shakes their hands. Dobson trips a little, on the edges of the podium, but he recovers.

"And now, ladies and gentlemen, the moment we've all been waiting for," says the principal a little too close to the microphone. "This year's $500 Lilith Cupworth Grant goes to …"

I wonder if my hair looks too goofy. If Sabine's dress is too short. My legs too white. Nona pushes her suddenly very strong hand against my back and I start to rise from my seat.

"Ms. Martha Hornbuckle." reads the principal off of the paper he peels from the hand of the art teacher.

Sabine says, *Holy cow.*

four

The refreshments table goes on for miles. Deli platters all fancied up with endive. A tiered cupcake server. Plastic bowls of M&Ms. Sushi that looks like it's been rolled in Rice Krispies. Immediately following the awards ceremony, I walk out of the cafetorium to hide in the hall behind the food. I can't face my parents or Nona or anyone. Martha included.

At the far end of the table there's some cheese and crackers. I grab a little paper plate and heap it with Ritz and mottled squares of Swiss and Colby. Goosebumps have sprouted on my arms. The red dress is too summery. I'm chilled.

My homeless guy and dog has been replaced by Martha's Mount Hood. I don't know what they did with my sketch. People are trickling out of the ceremony, like recently chastised grade school kids; they all walk with their heads down. Then, out in the hall, they become art patrons. They back up a bit, as though in a museum, stroking chins and clearing throats. My family is still making its way down the aisle. Martha seems to have disappeared.

My heart is beating fast. Why am I so upset? Why does my head and heart feel like they've just been smashed with a wooden club?

Ms. Bowerman is walking toward me. Quick, but trying to seem not quick. She looks right, left, over her shoulder, then grabs me and pulls me into an empty classroom. World History. There're colorful posters of Egyptians and a papier mâche Sphinx on a table near the window. Outside, it's dusk. Purple and rosy sky. A dark gray bank of cloud on the horizon. Something that would come out nice with an iPhone camera. Especially if you had one of those panorama apps.

"I tried calling you, Brady. Several times. I'm so sorry," says Ms. Bowerman.

The red dress clings to my thighs. I wish I had a sweater to cover my boobs.

"It's a legal thing, Brady. Ridiculous."

"A legal thing?" I'm in some parallel universe here. I have no idea what my art teacher is talking about.

"Counsel advised that offering you the prize would look like a bribe. Given the circumstances of your parents' pending lawsuit. But that's not what they told Cupworth."

Outside the door, the low conversations, some laughter, a saxophone starts up. Ms. Bowerman sees the puzzled look on my face. "The company line is, Brady Wilson is on academic probation, and is therefore ineligible."

"I am? On academic probation?"

"It doesn't help that you've been skipping class, Brady. And Mr. Garrison says he saw you getting high in the parking lot."

The retired-cop-hall-monitor guy? Saw me with Connor? "I don't really care about the damn scholarship. It's just, my parents. My grandparents. Putting them through this embarrassment. It's not fair."

Ms. Bowerman covers my scantily-clad self with an arm-over-the-shoulder. A hank of dreads scratches against my collarbone. "I know, Brady. It really sucks."

She whispers conspiratorially, "Giving the award to Martha? She's not a fraction the artist you are. I guess that's what bothers me more than anything."

Martha painted that picture from a postcard. The sort you can buy at the Japanese Garden gift shop. I remember that she wanted to get together with me afterwards. "Did she know?"

Ms. Bowerman doesn't want to tell me. She sighs, then says, "We had to make sure she was coming tonight."

Given that my heart feels like a million little needles just punctured it, Voodoo Doughnuts would be the perfect place to be right now.

Dusk has gone black outside. Only one bank of lights shines in this room, aimed at a scroll of hieroglyphics. A mobile of mummies hangs above us. Next year, this might be the only art the students of Greenmeadow get to do. Recreating history, one pyramid at a time. Maybe they could combine it with math class. Martha. She squeezed my hand in the cafetorium. She sat down next to me and my family and all the time, she knew?

"Oh, Brady, Honey. You poor thing."

Ms. Bowerman takes a crumpled napkin from the pocket of her parachute pants and dabs at my mascara-blackened tears.

"I can't go out there," I sniff. "Not yet."

"No, no, you can't, dear. Sit down. Give yourself a few minutes. I'll come back and get you once the crowd clears out a bit."

I want to tell her to let my parents and grandparents know where I am, but it would be worse to have them trudge in here all full of pity and disgust. I settle into one of the all-in-one-chair-desks and rest my forehead on my arms.

Bowerman turns out the light and the door clicks closed behind her.

I don't know how much time passes, but the next thing that happens is my shoulders are being rubbed, and a soft voice says, "You OK?"

I keep my eyes closed. Feign sleep. Be on your way, Brutus.

"I told your parents I'd take you home," says the voice of betrayal.

"I'll walk," I mumble into my arms.

"I have something else I need to talk to you about, Brady. You can't keep ditching me."

With that, I lurch up and knock into her chin. I turn around and she's rubbing her jaw. "Ditching you? I'm ditching you? Please."

"Sorry. Word choice. Bad. Let's start over."

I glare at her, this fake-tan Miss Greenmeadow who just (minutes? hours?) stood in my spotlight and received a ginormous poster with the words *five-hundred dollars* scripted across it. The words *Cupworth* and *Prize*.

"Of course, I want to share the money with you," she says. *Really?* Give me a break.

"The whole thing was so…complicated."

"I'm trying not to punch you in the face right now."

Martha grins.

"I didn't mean that figuratively."

"Do you want to slap me around while we're eating bacon maple bars?"

Bacon maple bars. As if a stupid doughnut will make everything OK again. Martha's face is so hopeful. She can't stand to have people mad at her. Even as a kid, the few times she got in trouble for talking during class, she'd spend recess helping the teacher straighten the coat closet or staple math worksheets together.

"I'm not stepping one foot outside this classroom until everyone is gone," I tell her. "Plus, you need to find me a sweater or something."

Martha and her thick, chestnut mane of hair, her perfect skin and C-cup boobs, nods. And because she's Martha, she peels her vegan leather jacket off her torso and drapes it around my shoulders. I sigh. I've been friends with Martha since first grade. I guess we're going to go get some doughnuts.

There's the usual line out the door and snaked along 3rd Avenue at the doughnut shop, where you can partake in pastries named for body parts, sex acts and super heroes. You can get married here, or have a funeral. If you're gay, you can have a commitment ceremony. Or if you're not, you still can. What Martha and I are doing, according to Martha, is having a counseling session. She's the counselor and I'm the patient. "Client," she corrects.

Martha wants to help me, she lets me know. To fix what's broken. To help me cope with *all the stuff you've been through*. She's good at it, too. One of those people with a natural gift for compassionate response.

Outside on the sidewalk, in a line filled with hipsters, she spits on her hand and smooths my green hair down. She steps back and takes me in, says I look amazing in Sabine's dress. Like a whole new person. I want to tell her about hearing my sister's voice, but something stops me. She says the doughnuts are her treat. *Duh*, I want to say.

"So, when *did* you know? About the Cupworth thingy."

Martha fiddles with her leather bracelet. "Yesterday," she admits. "That's why I was trying to get you to come have lunch at Norm's."

A breeze kicks up, and a crumpled Subway paper cup rolls down the middle of the road like a tumbleweed. "I can't believe nobody thought to contact my parents."

"Yeah, it's a raw deal. But, really, Brady, you can't let your life go down the toilet."

Her eyebrows are amazing when she says that. They form

this studied, concerned *V* that I thought you needed a therapy degree to pull off. "The toilet?"

"Of course you're grieving and upset, but even before Sabine, you were spiraling and antisocial. People were talking."

"And by people you mean …"

"You're so smart, Brady. So talented. I'd give anything to be able to draw like you. I just hate to see you slip down that slope. Y'know, like Connor and his ilk."

My back teeth clamp down, my hands curve into fists. Connor. How could she even mention that name around me? The image of his red eyes, the muscles rippling under his shirt slap up against the snotty way Martha just said *ilk*. As if Connor Christopher were a zombie or some evil being instead of a teenaged stoner who everyone suddenly hates. It's true that he's a total loser, but it bugs me the way Martha can be holier-than-thou sometimes.

"They gave me that award because you're flunking out, Brady. You're not turning in work, not showing up to class. You can point the finger at whomever you wish, but really, you need to take a good, long look in the mirror."

Martha's *Forever 21* faux leather tunic-jacket feels like a cold snake on my skin. My feet, all squished into Sabine's sandals, are throbbing. In line, we're inching closer to the Voodoo Doughnut door, where the promise of sugar and whimsy await. There's a band playing here tonight. A drum and electric guitar fighting for attention bursts into the cooling night air every time the door opens. Into the noise of it all I say, "They gave you the award, Martha, because they didn't want it to appear like they were trying to coerce my parents out of a lawsuit."

My best friend's forehead wrinkles in confusion.

"And besides," I add, before I can stop myself. "You shouldn't judge people. Connor included. What do you even know about him, anyway?"

"The boy who killed your sister? You're defending him?"

I sense the entire line of doughnut patrons stopping mid-text at this statement.

"I'm not defending him," I half-whisper.

"Connor was baked. You know that. He missed his cue, and Sabine's neck broke because of it."

Ms. Bowerman and *the company line* statement pops up in my brain. Yes, that's what we all bought into—Connor was high and he fucked up. But something about Martha's snippy tone tonight, and the way this whole Cupworth thing went down, and how I'm not so sure about anything anymore, I'm wondering what I'm doing out here, in the doughnut line, with this person. I'm about to ask her to loan me bus fare, when she says, "And, Brady, there's something else I need to tell you."

"What, are you like the new Portland Public Superintendent or School Board President or something?"

"This won't be easy."

I just glare at her, this self-appointed therapist so-called friend of mine.

"It's Nick."

"Nick?"

"Nick and I," says Martha. "We're seeing each other."

A piece of garbage blows up against my bare leg thanks to a cold, gusty wind that's now turned the weather back to Portland in the spring. I shiver in Sabine's dress, and wrap Martha's jacket tighter around me.

five

This is Sabine. Have a great day.

Her greeting sounds more tentative, distant, as if the greeting has been re-recorded by someone pretending to be my sister. "Everything's going to shit," I say into my little speaker of my cell, into the voicemail void. The tree that falls in the forest that no one will hear.

The black of my room is lit up only by the pinprick light from my phone. A violent rain beats against my window, but other than that, there's the no sound of 2:00 a.m. "Where are you?" I ask Sabine.

I'm still wearing her Juicy Couture, the soft cotton blend of it hugging my ribs. Nona's blanket is a cocoon over the dress and I'm hoping I'll wake up as a butterfly tomorrow. Or one of those spectacular moths that spins silk. *Don't be such a drama queen,* says Sabine in my ear like a bullet. And, as if she orchestrated an accompaniment, a branch from the azalea bush outside my window scrapes against the glass.

If I was a moth, I could flutter around light bulbs all night then collapse my wings together into a wafer come daylight. Tuck myself into a closet. Eat some wool. Contemplate the layers of betrayal that the human heart is capable of. I dial Sabine again. The immediate voicemail, her greeting *This is Sabine.* The bossy demand, *Have a great day.* And into the vacuum I say, "Martha is dating Nick, Sabine. What the hell is up with that?"

Thank God Mom and Dad were asleep by the time I got home. After the embarrassment of the art show, the last thing I wanted was to process the whole thing with them. I'm sure it'll come up in the grief counseling session next week. The counselor will ask us all how we feel. Mom will be furious. Dad will be sad. We'll use I-statements like the quick-study grief clients we are. We'll yank the Kleenexes from his lacquered tissue box and dab at the corners of our eyes. On Dad's insurance we have eight free sessions, and so far we've used three. As the hole of time opens wider and wider between Sabine's death and our continuing lives, we'll fit in five more grief counseling sessions. A season. A summer. Christmas. If I were a moth, I'd chew that hole bigger, feeding on the things that keep me going. But I'm not a moth. I'll never be a moth. "I'm going to skip school tomorrow," I tell Sabine's voicemail.

I wake up with the phone in my hand and Nona's blanket corded around my neck. It's morning, and too late for me to get to school on time, so there's no hurry. Rain drains down the gutter outside sounding like a toilet running. My phone's on silent and I see I've missed three calls and eleven texts. The texts are mostly from Martha and I delete them without reading. The ones from Mom say, *Hope you get up in time for school*, and *Sorry about last night. Let's debrief later.* One from Dad says, *Beach house bound after work. Pack a bag.*

We haven't been to the beach house yet. Our last trip was Thanksgiving, when we were still two parents and two kids. One big unhappy, yet intact, family. What would we have done differently had we known that one of us would be dead in a few months? Maybe Dad wouldn't have spent the whole weekend watching football. Maybe I would have been less snarky about playing endless games of hearts with Nona and Nono. Maybe I would have been kinder about Nick being part of the weekend. Nick and his sly feeling-up-my-sister-under-the-blanket-in-the-living-room moves. Her giggling and squeaking in that girl way. I wish I could take back my eye-rolling. Nick. Martha. And what does *seeing* mean, anyway? Are they doing it? Is Martha, Patron Saint of Pity Favors, giving my dead sister's boyfriend hand jobs in the front seat of her car?

The morning is half over already. I'd be done with trig and art and now I'd be in world history, taking a test I haven't studied for. Before this term, I'd been rocking a 3.5. Now? I'd be lucky to not fail everything. Ms. Bowerman's folded arms. Her bushy eyebrows, concern lined into her forehead, she'd be disappointed if I flunked out. She, who just last month had written me a stellar recommendation for San Francisco Art Institute's Precollege Summer Program.

I crawl out of bed and stumble out to the kitchen, where the crumbled Voodoo Doughnuts bag sits like a centerpiece to last night's series of misfortunes. The maple bacon bar is stale when I pull it out, a shingle of diarrhea-colored glaze slides off and splinters on the tile floor. Sabine loved these. She could eat three in a sitting before vomiting the calories down the toilet.

My sister was crazy for food. As a little girl she'd moan orgasmically while savoring Nona's homemade bread, Mom's rhubarb cobbler. I'd seen her go through an entire pizza, just herself. Pork down a pound of BBQ ribs, licking her plate at the end to get at every bit of sauce like a retriever. Whatever she'd inhale, she'd burn it all off. Until a few years ago when her height leveled off at five-foot-eight and her ass started to pad up. "Cheerleaders can't be fat," she'd whine, and then weep like a widow. Then she discovered how she could have her cake and eat it too. So to speak.

My sister did everything big, with her whole heart. A

cheerleading natural, her gritty alto voice belting out G R E E N M E A D O W letter by letter. You didn't always see it in her, but she was tough. If you got up in her business on the wrong day, she'd go all laser tongue and cut your heart out. I cram the nubby end of the doughnut in my mouth robustly, like Sabine would, and in my head she approves with her signature, *Atta girl, Midge.*

There's a list of things to pack for this weekend lying on the kitchen table. Trader Joe's items: white bean hummus and dark chocolate almonds. Some of that premade bagged salad with cranberries and walnuts and little globs of goat cheese. Spanakopita, Sabine's favorite comfort food, is scratched out. The remaining Wilsons do not like cooked spinach. So I guess it's settled. We're officially "getting away." Our therapist will be pleased.

Outside, it's sheets of rain. Where yesterday's warm, sunny weather had lawn mowers firing off, today's more typical April skies leave the streets and parks empty. This is perfect, since it appears that I am now officially cutting school. Amid the last sugary crumbs of the doughnut, an idea blossoms in my head. I need a solitary road trip before tonight's family road trip. This idea includes me taking Sabine's car out for a spin. A whole movie plays in my brain, one that features a ride through Kaady Car Wash—the premium offering that includes a liquid polish spray. At the very least, I'd get the bird shit rubbed off with those jiggling chamois sponge-strips.

In a few minutes, I'm dressed and have the car keys in hand. I'm licenseless and permitless, but that hasn't stopped me from several emergency designated-driver runs when Sabine was too wasted to drive. I can almost see the old Volvo smile, its headlights greeting me as I approach and then squeak the heavy driver's side door open.

Inside though, it looks like an interrupted day. A mostly

empty Starbucks Venti-sized paper cup with Sabine's lipstick marks on the white plastic lid pokes up from the cup holder. Two notebooks and World of Chemistry lie in a stack on the passenger seat. It still smells like my sister in here. That damp, perfumy smell with a little spearmint mixed in. The engine makes a kachung-kachung-kachung sound before bursting to life. The car shakes a little, and then settles into its Volvo purr. The wipers smear the rain across the windshield as I back out of the drive and head out onto the road toward town. *I miss that car*, says Sabine, her voice dimmer and sadder than usual.

I drive up into the hills a bit, my hands at ten and two as though following some lesson from a driver's ed class I've yet to take. I pass all the houses of all kids I've gone to school with forever. Sabine's teammates on the cheer squad, girls I once played soccer with. I'm heading to the big cell tower behind Martha's house, where, if it's clear, you can see both Mt. Saint Helens and Mt. Hood. But it's far from clear today. Little mud creeks run down the shoulders of the road as I head up. Bright green fern fronds and glowing moss jut off of the occasional downed log. There are no sidewalks in our part of town, and many roads are gravel, pocked with potholes. As much as everyone complains, they choose to live here in this seemingly rural countryside a few minutes from the center of downtown. When the city threatens to assess improvements and charge homeowners for curbs and gutters, there's always uproar. Petitions, meetings, and brouhahas. Ergo, the goat paths.

I guide Sabine's car around a couple of branches and some chunky rocks from a little mudslide that must have just happened. Ahead of me are the fancy iron gates that grace Martha's house. I know the code. I could just press the keypad and, voila, I'd be in the Hornbuckle compound, where a pair of mastiffs often lope about as though protecting a castle. Martha is a wealthy girl. Logging money from decades of clear-cutting, which her liberal, environmentally progressive parents justify through foundation activity that claims to be saving some rare species of butterfly. Martha getting the $500 Cupworth scholarship is like Bill Gates winning a computer. Ridiculous on so many levels. The compound looks empty today. Her parents might be off on one of their cruises, leaving Martha to manage the staff around her extracurricular schedule. What would I do inside the Martha estate if I were to trespass? Short sheet her bed? Pull up the carefully planted tulips so lovingly tended by a crew of Hispanic gardeners? I drive past the entry, past the ginormous tree house where Sabine and I enjoyed many a summer sleepover, and then U-turn at her neighbor's driveway.

In middle school, Martha hungered after my sister like a drooling groupie. If Sabine showed up wearing plaid boxers over eggplant leggings, the next day, there Martha would be in the exact same ensemble. I didn't blame her though; everyone wanted to be Sabine. And Martha being Martha, she'd come around eventually. Call me up on a rainy Saturday and invite me to help her ladle chili at the soup kitchen.

Back in first grade, on the playground one day, a bigger girl, a schoolyard bully-type girl, pulled Martha's bright pink jeans down, revealing her *Finding Nemo* underpants. There was little Martha, crying and trying to pull her pants back up, and the bully girl laughing and calling her a retard. I didn't even think about it. I just walked up and kicked that bully girl in her big butt.

By then the teachers were onto what was going on and the bully girl got suspended and Martha threw her arms around me, and that was that.

We grew apart in middle school, but the last couple of years, Martha has had a renewed interest in me. Maybe it's the art thing; maybe it's just that she needs a break from all the intense competition with the popular girls. Don't know. But I always seem to say *sure* when she invites me to do something.

The first time I ever smoked weed was in Martha's tree house one August night. It was my 15th birthday, and Martha had invited me to a Wicked Tail concert to which her dad secured backstage passes. Our hopes were pinned on getting the lead singer, Hurricane Blu, to autograph our skin, but after the show he'd been whisked away, and the only people backstage were roadies and a few stoners who were friends of friends of friends. This ghostly boy with purple hair gave Martha a pinner in exchange for her teeth marks on his shoulder. She'd shrugged and bit down through the flesh just above his collarbone until a little trickle of blood pooled into a bruise under his skin there. Martha being Martha, she asked if he wanted one on the other side to match. He winked at her and told her next time, sure, and he slipped the weed into the front of her bra.

We lit that twisted paper and watched it glow and die a few times before one of us was brave enough to suck on it. Under the rubbery leaves of the magnolia, lying on smooth plank flooring most people would only use for their actual homes, Martha and I got high. Well, sort of high. The burning pot scorched the lining of my throat, and I coughed and coughed, and then, suddenly, everything seemed hilarious. A strand of Martha's gleaming hair that caught itself between two branches, the way she made her eyebrows "V," the sound of her voice feigning a Southern accent, *Whah Brady, I do believe you're stoned. Now what would your mama think?* All of that rolled to a boil in the laugh center of my brain. Now, the tree house is gray and splintery after the wet winter. Littered with dead leaves.

I drive back down the hill, and the rain turns to ice pellets. Little balls of hail like Styrofoam bullets spray down on everything. Ping, ping, ping, ping. The wipers propel the icy mess across the windshield smearing up my view, and there's no good reason why I should push my luck and continue on. None. And yet, I do. At the fork where I could follow the twists back down the hill toward home, I hairpin back up, toward the vast expanse of Forest Park, and its endless trails. Not too long ago a man and his young daughter lived in the woods of Forest Park for years before their camp was found. The man had home-schooled her, and the campsite was stocked with textbooks and writing implements. The authorities took the girl into protective custody, and her father fled, but as soon as the girl was in a foster home, she escaped and found her father again. I always loved that story.

The tiny bit of latte remaining in Sabine's Starbucks cup sloshes around; little stop-sign shaped bits of mold lap up onto the cardboard and make a bright green ring. As the car climbs the hill, the icy pellets grow bigger and fiercer. A fog separating the warm inside of the Volvo from the almost freezing outside adds to my near-blindness. Up here, on this road, in a small farmhouse-looking bungalow is where Connor Christopher lives. I know this, and somehow can't stop myself from aiming Sabine's car in its direction. Sabine has no comment, though I'm straining to hear one. The Chemistry textbook slides off the seat as I take a corner too rough. I overcorrect, and now the tires on the right side of the car are in a ditch. There is a sound of rubber sliding through mud, and then the car shifts and the moldy latte tips over and green slime spills all over my shoe, which is pumping, pumping the brake. Ahead of me is a car length of mud before a straight drop onto someone's roof and I pump harder, wondering if the last words out of my mouth will be *fuck*, or *no*, or *holy shit*. I think about my parents having to plan yet another memorial service, about my soul joining Sabine's in the green room of heaven while Nona prays the rosary to get us on the big stage. I think about our cell phone greetings, the two dead Wilson girls and how now, for sure, *60 Minutes* would do an exposé on Greenmeadow High.

I blast the horn for no reason. What am I thinking? That the slippery bank will get out of the way and be replaced by a bale of cotton? Mud and hail splatter the windshield as my tires grind deep and I smell the smell of hot brakes. I hear the crackle of stiff blackberry vines. The car veers and lurches and skids to a stop against the thick trunk of a fir. I uncramp my fingers from the steering wheel where they've turned whiter than the hail. The heavens have opened up. Sabine's frozen tears pelt down on the roof of her car so hard it's like I'm inside of a pinball machine.

Nice job, she says into the cacophony.

I'm aware of the strange vibrato of my heart. Actual fear. Something happening to my body. It dawns on me that I'm not dead, and the relief of revising my funeral scenario spreads like honey from my scalp to my toes. Right outside the window is the precipitous drop into a rich person's backyard. There's the outdoor kitchen, the fire pit, the greenhouse, the elaborate swing set, all Street of Dreams perfect and un-intruded upon by a 1990 Volvo and that poor, grieving Wilson girl. My fear turns to elation. To aliveness. A second chance at grace and whatever it is that born-agains sing about.

But there's a wee problem. I seem to have slid off into a ditch and the car is buried under a rind of frozen slush.

Once the hailstorm passes, I yawn the door open and step out into the ridges of muck. Steam is lifting off of the car like a halo. The tires are halfway sunk. There's a little wrinkle in the license plate where it's gnawing the tree. I realize that when I conceived of this road trip I didn't envision myself outside, actually, so I'm ridiculously underdressed in a jeans jacket and leggings and my Keds with the holes in the toe, now splashed with moldy latte. I've also left my cell at home. There aren't too many options beyond pounding on one of these McMansion doors and convincing the maid to let me call—who? Mom? Dad? Martha?

There is another option, of course. The other student at Greenmeadow most likely to be cutting class. The boy who didn't catch my sister. The wastoid pariah who is probably doing bong hits while *Wheel of Fortune* airs on a flat screen in his living room, which happens to be located just around the bend. Maybe it's not as long a walk as I think to get back to my house? Sabine's icy tears have stopped, and the transient blue April sky is hatching above. I give it fifteen, maybe twenty minutes before the next onslaught. Cold wet is already wicking into the canvas of my sneakers. I take a deep breath and head uphill, toward Connor Christopher's bungalow.

Bunches of bright daffodils rising from lime-green thickets flank the flagstone in front of Connor's house. Some are those double-bloom types with the deepest egg-yolky center surrounded by white or chick-yellow. A few are freakishly long and slender—Jack-and-the-beanstalk daffodils that point skyward. Fluorescent moss dots the path, invading any crack or opening. A fat banana slug slimes along the stone. A pile of hail is melting just ahead of it. I always try to step around the slugs and moss of the forest, but here at Connor's house, I'm tempted to stomp all over anything that seeks to live. I envision yanking the flowers up, bulbs and all, and hurling them down the hill. Why have I come? Wouldn't it be better to court hypothermia than to trespass on the grounds of an outlaw?

A shiver crawls along my back sideways from shoulder to shoulder. I rap the solid Christopher door with my frozen knuckles. The house greets me with stillness. There's no evidence that anyone is home. No light on inside. No sounds of feet on flooring. Only a few months ago Connor's family hosted the annual squad fundraiser. They had a catchy name. *Raising Cheer*. They auctioned off a bunch of booze and beach house vacations and made about twenty grand. My parents had offered our Manzanita house for a week this summer. The Christophers won the bid. And here I am again, with the next no-degrees-of-separation coincidence. But it looks like my knock will go unanswered, so, hugging the chill from my ribs, I turn around and start back down the flagstones to the potholed road. Clouds are moving in again as I jog-walk back to the car. Maybe I'll warm up for a few minutes in front of the ancient half-working defroster before walking down the hill to my house.

My toes are getting numb as I round the bend toward the sunken Volvo. My shoes are caked in clumped slime. If I were in school right now, it'd almost be over. Last period. Literature. We're reading *As I Lay Dying*. The irony is not lost on me as I plod down the hill. Now I see it, the poor car that is, at least, no longer covered in bird shit. And beside the car, peering into its foggy windows, is Connor Christopher.

"Hey," I say just like that. *Hey*. As if.

"Brady," he says, all startled and confused.

His eyes are the usual bloodshot. He's wearing a hoodie, shorts and running shoes. Dressed even less weather-appropriate than me.

"What, were you thinking that Sabine drove this up here?"

I don't know what made me say that. I'm not usually so creepy. Connor straightens up, looks past me, then back at the car, then at the darkening sky. "It's gonna dump any minute," he says in his deep, honey-toned voice. *Faulkner*, I think. *That's probably what Faulkner sounds like.*

As if by magic, the first pellets of hail unload at his command. Inside my head Sabine says, *What, you both too stupid to know when to get out of the rain?* There's not much else to do but climb in. Connor and me both, crawling over the moldy latte and the chem text and the notebooks.

We sit there in silence as the shower of ice continues. He smells like boy. A faint scent of Axe mixed with mud. And because it's Connor, there's that whiff of weed. Me in the passenger seat, and him in the driver's. As though we're on a date. A couple of truants. All we need is a six of PBR. Into the growing awkward I say, "You don't have, like, AAA or anything, do you?"

"I didn't know you had a license."

"Who says I do?"

He nods. "I can get my stepdad's truck. Pull this out."

"I sort of hoped for something like that. I, um, actually went to your house just now."

He turns his head now. Looks at me with squinched up forehead lines. "I heard about the whole art award thing."

Facebook, no doubt. The town crier. I shrug. And then I notice something glimmering in the little hoodie shadow against Connor Christopher's face. A familiar trinket. A cross with a tiny sapphire in the middle, dangling from his earlobe. Mutely, I point to it, and Connor reaches his thumb and fingers around it, rubbing it like a greedy person referring to money.

"How'd you get that?"

"She gave it to me."

Alliances and partnerships and secret handshakes—so many things happening under my nose. Why would my sister give Connor Christopher her earring?

As if reading my face, he says, "It's complicated."

"I'm beginning to think that I'm the one who died. And

I'm in that limbo my grandparents always talk about, where nothing makes any sense at all."

He says, "That why you're not in school today?"

"I overslept."

"Yeah. A lot of that going around I guess."

He doesn't pursue. Doesn't ask what I'm doing up here. A little sigh comes out my mouth. I feel my shoulders sink. Relaxation. Rest. It's nice. So, into that space I throw a wrench. "Did you know Martha's seeing Nick?"

He doesn't answer me right away. And then, his voice is real quiet when he says, "It's not exactly news, Brady."

"Yeah, well, it was to me."

The hail stops as though someone flipped a switch. My feet are resting on World of Chemistry, making jagged mud prints on top of the picture of the test tube. "I thought I was going over the bank. Curtains."

"You came close."

"It was like, in those five seconds, my brain spun out the whole thing. My parents getting the call from the EMTs, planning my service. More ashes. More rosaries and mass cards."

I hear Connor swallow hard.

"You have no idea what it's like to have her as your sister. You start to believe in destiny. You start to believe in the grand plan. She got everything, everything she went after."

"Not everything," Connor says.

His green eyes are flecked with amber. His eyebrows thick as wooly caterpillars. His fingers are wrapped around the steering wheel, pulsing nervously.

"So, you think you can pull this out?"

He nods. "We should do it quick. Before, you know…"

I do know. This situation? Me and Connor and Sabine's precariously positioned car? Neither of us wants to have to explain it. I wouldn't know where to begin.

*   *   *

By the time we trudge back up to Connor's house and he plunges into every one of his stepdad's coat pockets, and by the time he finally comes up with a spare hanging from a nail in his garage, finds the right rope, and gets the truck started, it's after school already. Several more hail bursts have delivered more semi-frozen mess, and when we rumble down the lane to Sabine's car, it's another few inches sunken down—that much closer to falling into the Street of Dreams backyard.

"You stay here," he tells me, bringing the Ford F-250 to a stop a few feet from the Volvo's bumper. I'm not going to argue. Connor slides out the door, leaving it half open, the engine running, grabs the rope and loops the heavy sisal on a hook underneath the car. Me, I would have wrapped it around the bumper and it would have yanked right off. Watching him through the rainy back window loop and tie and do all those boyscouty things makes me sad. Before the accident, Connor was popular—if a little fringy. He was Sabine's lift partner—she's the one who convinced him to abandon wrestling for cheering. My sister could persuade a super model to gain seventy-five pounds and learn to throw shot put. That's how she was. Everyone knew Connor had a crush on her. Half the boys, no, maybe ninety percent of the boys had a crush on Sabine.

"It's in neutral," he tells me when he climbs back in, his hoodie all sopping wet.

I nod. Neutral. Another thing I wouldn't have thought about.

He throws the truck in gear and edges forward and I hear the sucking sound of tires in heavy mud. I feel us being pulled at from behind, the engine straining. Connor says, "C'mon, Baby," low and whispery with his Faulknery voice.

The Volvo wiggles out, and then slips a little left, right, now an entire wheel is hanging off the edge, but the rest of the car is freed and following the pickup down the street. "Yes." I half yell.

We ease to a stop, our little caravan, and then Connor pulls the parking brake and climbs back out to undo the rope. Our adventure is over. The car is unstuck and safe. Instead of the total relief I should feel, I'm a little let down. Wishful that it could have been a bit more complicated, somehow. I realize that I, too, am damp, and I start to shiver a little getting out of the truck.

By the time I reach the door of the car, Connor has looped the rope back up and thrown it into his truck bed. I'm not quite sure what to say, but something automatically comes out my mouth. "Our secret, right?"

Connor turns around, folds his arms. Sabine's earring flashes in a bolt of sudden sunlight. Fitting, for Good Friday. "Won't be putting this on Facebook, or anything," he says.

"I owe you one," I tell him. "Seriously. At least, maybe I should have your phone number. We could get coffee or doughnuts or something sometime. My treat."

He shrugs, scribbles his number on a piece of rolling paper, and hands it to me. The sky, all brilliant gunmetal, highlights a magenta azalea bush right behind him. The incredible beauty of it stops me cold. That's the thing about art. You have no control over when it shows up and bursts your heart into splinters. This time of year screams with cruel beauty. You can't go anywhere without being attacked by it. I realize then, that I owe him an apology. For yesterday's—was it really just yesterday?—*fuck off*. I'm thinking about how to say I'm sorry, but I take too long. Connor's already in the truck, pulling onto the goat path road, the mud flaps on his dad's truck waving goodbye.

six

The summer before my freshman year, after Sabine's first year of high school, Dad had a midlife crisis. In family therapy we refer to that summer, three years ago, as Johnsaffair. As if the entire season, the June, July, August of it had been replaced by a ninety-day month called Johnsaffair. An anomaly, like a leap year that only happened once. But Mom will not let it go. Nothing in our house has been the same since.

The woman who had a starring role in Johnsaffair was a fitness model for Nike, where Dad and pretty much everyone in suburban Portland work. She was seventeen years younger than Dad, but without makeup she was plain, sort of mannish. Her golf game was better than Dad's, and she was a ranked tennis pro. Her name was Natalie.

When Mom found some weird receipts in Dad's wallet, he confessed right away. I can still hear the scream that came out of the kitchen that night. The shrill piercing of a cat being squashed by a linebacker wearing an army boot. Sabine and I were watching *The Bachelor* reruns in the family room, and then all hell broke loose. Casserole dishes against cupboards. An entire closet of sports jackets flung out the front door. Mom and her Italian temper. Dad's car keys hurled against the big living room window and the spider crack that happened because of it.

Sabine came over to my La-Z-Boy and we squished in together like kittens, while above us, a flurry of angry words.

Mom's voice: Never. Fucking. Believe.

Dad's voice: The girls, Sonia.

Mom's voice: Get used to it.

Dad's voice: Talk. Love. Calm.

Mom's voice: Out. Never. Don't think that.

Dad's voice: Reason. Work this out. For the best.

Mom's voice: Cheat. Lies. Dead.

And on it went, Sabine and I quiet until she said, "I knew about it."

I still didn't know what they were fighting about. I thought maybe Dad had lost money in the stock market, or something was wrong with Nona and Dad had been insensitive. But they'd never fought this way before. "About what?"

"Natalie," she said. "I saw them out together. They didn't see me. But I saw them, you know, kissing."

"Natalie? Who's Natalie?"

"Dad's girlfriend. His lover."

The word *lover* rolled off my sister's tongue like a foreign thing. As though she'd said *Amiga*, over pronouncing it with a fake accent.

"Mom'll kick him out," Sabine said. "I know it."

That night was like when I was eight, the only girl in second grade who still believed in Santa. Cathi Serge set me straight on the jungle gym when I asked her if she'd written her letter to Santa Claus yet. The steely hard truth clunking down from a cloud to smash the fancy dream apart. "Oh, Brady, you don't still *believe*, do you?"

That early June night, it was another betrayal. My parents had other lives besides being parents. My heart felt pried open; moths flew out. I put my hands over my ears like the "hear no evil" monkey as the crashing and shouting and sobbing above us continued into the night. Sabine put her arm around me. We tugged Nona's black afghan tight around us, making an Irish twin cocoon, my fingers and toes crossed for luck.

*   *   *

Our little beach house is slicked with moss when we get there late Friday afternoon. That's what I notice before anything else. A green slime coating glows from the wood steps and the deck that wraps around the cottage. The ancient iron gate to the hot tub, styled with four daisies on top—one for each of us—hangs off of a hinge. A pool of rust marks the concrete beneath it. My parents sigh in tandem as we pull to a stop in the drive.

Thick, salty fog hugs the house, and us, as we make our way inside, lugging overnight bags and groceries from New Seasons. Mom has iPod buds in her ears like a sullen teenager as she shepherds a Ziploc baggie filled with a handful of Sabine's ashes to the gas stove mantel. Dad sets the sack of staples on the counter, and before even putting them away, he pours a glass of something amber-colored. I scramble up to the loft, to the futon room, where there's an array of DVDs and a bookcase full of romance novels. "Want a drink?" I hear Dad call. Mom doesn't respond.

The only other time I've been the single daughter here is when Sabine was away at cheerleading camp a couple of Augusts ago, and my parents and I came out for the week. It was a work week—Mom was determined to erase any trace of Natalie from all surfaces. She brought new linens, paint. She even swapped out the dishes, claiming we needed an upgrade. But I knew it was about punishing Dad. She cracked the whip the entire time, presenting list after list: clean the gutters, empty and refill the hot tub, scrub the deck. We were vanquishing Johnsaffair the way people burn sage. But more first-gen Italian American wife than Native American. Penance beyond a Hail Mary. A new bed was delivered to the master. One with fancy controllers to dial in firmness. Sleep numbers.

"Sunset in twenty minutes," calls Dad now, on this Good Friday. Sunset. Hardly. Maybe a tiny sliver of red on the horizon, but it's a ritual, walking the strip of beach to town and back as afternoon sinks into evening. Sun or no sun, it's what we do. And this evening we're going to do it with some of my sister's cremains.

Seagulls screech, and a curved line of pelicans descends into the surf when we get to the ocean. It's a herring run, and the three of us stop to watch the big, brown birds dive and scoop up the tiny fish into their pouchy bills. Dad points to a young bird that is pick-pocketing an adult. "Spring," he says. "The season of generosity."

I nod. "Easter bounty."

Dad holds up the baggie of shards and fragments, as though lifting a young child for a better view of something.

Mom hugs her ribs. She's wearing a shearling jacket and matching deerskin hat. She says, all wistful, "What would it be like. To be a seabird?"

We're quiet for a few moments, gazing out at the spectacle of feeding frenzy. The pelicans lift and lower. Like cheerleaders. All together. Choreographed perfection. Riding the tide, then beating their massive wings, and rising, rising, hovering, and then crashing down again, the "U" of them. Standing at the water's edge with my parents, I decide that my sister has joined those birds. If it's true what Nona says, and she's waiting for her call from God from that green room limbo place, knowing Sabine, she's not just sitting there. She's with these pelicans, one eye on us, her former family. Maybe she sees the baggie of ashes dangling from Dad's fingertips. Her bill full of herring. Hungry, as always.

"I imagine," I say, answering Mom's rhetorical question,

"it's like being a cheerleader."

I feel the breath of Mom locked in her throat. The shards of her own heart just like the ashes in Dad's grip. My words hit her ears different than I meant them to. "Brady," she says under her breath.

"Shall we?" says Dad, unzipping the bag with a fingernail.

Mom puts her hand on top of Dad's. Not in a loving way. "No."

"We have to do it sometime, Sonia. Bit by bit, like we discussed."

"Not. Yet."

Most of my sister is still in the Asian urn in our living room. This is just a start. Somewhere to begin. "Why not, Mom? Isn't this why we're here?"

Mom turns to face me. "I'm not sure why we're here, exactly."

"We need to all be in agreement," Dad says, resealing Sabine.

The pelicans lift again, and fly off in a brown curl. Full from fish, ready to head to their nests for the night. The fog has lifted too, as it often does at the edge of the evening.

"It's getting late," says Dad. "Almost 7:30. I'm starving."

"Fish on Good Friday," I offer. "Should we go to the Clam Shanty in town?"

Nobody agrees out loud, but our footfalls continue on, leaving a pattern in the wet sand behind us. Waves lap near our feet. Rising tide will erase us soon. Then, out of nowhere, the image of Connor's face shrouded in hoodie forms in my mind. The glimmer of Sabine's crucifix earring against the fold of cloth. I close my eyes and can smell him, Sabine's best friend. Her partner. The boy who knows. The boy my parents blame.

By the time we reach the main drag, it's dusk. We wander up Laneda Street with the few tourists and second-home people who have come to spend Easter weekend at the coast. There's the cheap taco place, the expensive taco place, and the local watering hole. Three espresso shops, all closed for the night. A grocery store. The library. A used bookstore and a bakery. Realty offices with their laminated photos of beachfront in the windows. We always stop and browse the enticing descriptions, mostly so Dad can see if the beach house he got such a great deal on is still appreciating. The second-home market is in the ditch, the economy below water, still. Dad sighs as we pass the evidence: New Low Price, Owner Motivated, Short Sale, all typed in red block letters under pictures of custom beach homes. Ours is a shack by comparison. Not really an investment. More like a retreat.

We walk on. Mom's shearling beaded with the dew of nightfall. The kite store. The pet store. The whimsical jewelry place where Sabine and I once shoplifted a necklace, and then, guilt-ridden, secretly returned it.

Manzanita is the one beach town on the Oregon coast that runs perpendicular to the ocean rather than boardwalk parallel. Which is, according to my parents, what makes it special? There's less college kid hooligan cruising. Less cotton candy and tee-shirt hucksters. Unlike the towns slightly north—Cannon Beach, Seaside—Manzanita has a dearth of saltwater taffy for sale.

But there's the Clam Shanty. Known for razor clams and chowder and oyster shooters with handcrafted hot sauce. Sabine could eat a dozen-and-a-half in one sitting. A whole lemon sliced up thin, the way you do for tequila. She'd squeeze that lemon all over the jiggly oyster, dollop of sauce, then, raise the oval shell high, as though proposing a toast. The face she made when the fish slid down her throat. Repulsion and elation all at once. The same face she had when, one night, high on weed, she described what it's like to give a boy a blowjob.

The fish place is clearing out when we get there. The sidewalks roll up early in Manzanita. A disgruntled counter girl sighs as the bell on the door announces us. She's Saran-wrapping the deli goods, and I watch as her head sinks into her shoulders. No doubt she has after-work plans. I feel sorry for her, but annoyed. Last summer, when I worked at the Grill and Scoop in Beaverton, I never let it show how pissed off I was when last-minute customers came in. My waitress smile was solid. Professional. Poker face Brady.

Besides, we know what we want. This won't take long. Chowder and sour dough.

"For here or to go?" says the counter girl whose nametag claims she's Sam.

"We'll eat here," says Dad, and the girl lets out another sigh.

She's already put the chowder in the walk-in. She marches off, behind strips of plastic, and comes out bearing a steam pan between two thick mitts.

We sit down at one of the red-checkered oilcloth picnic tables, a waxy cup of fountain soda wedged in my hand. Mom and her herbal tea. We hear the beep-beep-whir of the microwave being engaged. The sawing of our bread. Dad twists the metal cap off of a Hefeweizen. "Cheers," he says.

Later, back at the beach house, alone on my futon and wrapped up in a Nona quilt, the gulls' screeching keeps replaying in my head. I can see those pelicans on the vast horizon, the gray and foam Pacific that goes on forever. On canvas, I'd choose thick, burnt gobs of sienna. Umber. English red. The tiniest stroke of cadmium yellow. Indigo and warm gray and a dab of French ultramarine. And then, a different painting. Azaleas, like the ones from earlier, all quinacridone magenta, sap green foliage against the cerulean sky. And Connor, half-hidden, but not. Connor Christopher, interrupting my vision of the ocean and the bushes and springtime. The earring, Sabine's dangling jewel.

Sabine. All my meanderings come back to her.

We're too far from the beach to hear the waves crash against sand and rock, but in my head, they do. The rhythm of it all is my heart. I want to hear her voice again tonight. Just once.

I reach for my phone. Press 3 on the speed dial. I want to hear the *This is Sabine. Have a great day.*

Instead, what I hear is the computer-voice of a robot saying, "The voice mailbox of the person you're trying to reach is full."

No.

Can't be.

All the messages falling in the forest. Hanging out in limbo, never to be heard by Sabine. I don't know her voicemail password. Why don't I know it? All of a sudden, in the deep night of my thoughts, I have a mission. To unlock Sabine's voice mailbox. To know who is still talking to her. What they're saying. Is Martha still calling her up? Is Nick? Is Connor? Mom? Dad? Nona?

I press in her number again, and follow the prompts. Try a code. Another code. Her birthday. Nick's birthday. Our address. Still, it's the computer voice telling me that the mailbox has reached its capacity.

I get up and climb down the loft ladder to use the bathroom, but the door is closed and I hear the whispering voice of Mom inside. Why is she in the guest bathroom? Who is she talking to? I sink down against the wall, crouched there, curious. My ear against the hollow door. "That's really sweet of you," I hear her say. "Yes, I'd love that."

Then, Dad's snoring from the master bedroom. Lately, it's

like a buzz saw with Dad. Mom whispers, "Maybe Wednesday. Or, if I come home early Sunday."

Then, "I'm not sure."

And, "Can't wait."

I tip-toe back up the ladder to the futon, the phone cradled in my hand like a brick I want to hurl through glass. I am sick to death of secrets. I am tired of never knowing the truth. I wish I had the nerve to call Connor is what I'm thinking as I drift off to sleep.

Seven

Duplicity, Mrs. McConnell writes on the board, underlining the word three times and following it with several dots of punctuation. "Faulkner's work is full of it. Exploring betrayal from many, many points of view. *As I Lay Dying*, ladies and germs, is awash with the theme."

Duplicity. The form of that word, the sound of it, is lyrical, beautiful. I loop the letters across my notebook.

"The interface between existence and the next thing—the hereafter, or the cessation of consciousness, these are all the themes our Faulkner explored," Mrs. McConnell continues. "Heavy stuff."

It's after lunch and warmish outside. The classroom windows face south. Heads are on desks. Some students are completely asleep, and the boy next to me has a thin line of drool pooling under his cheek. Mrs. McConnell is known for her death obsession. Her "Classics in Context" lit class will probably be cut next year, because it's controversial. Last grading period we read De Beauvoir's *She Came to Stay*, and I couldn't shake the death of the character, Francois, from my memory: *On the bed there still remained a living form, but it was already no one.*

"Faulkner was a post-structuralist, ladies and germs," says Mrs. McConnell. "By which I mean he explored matters of religion and religious truth." Her fingers make invisible quotation marks when she says truth.

"Duplicity, infidelity, God and the question of God, mortality, class and race theory, all classic Faulknerian themes that fuel this story about the death of matriarch Addie Bundren."

There is a wave of laughter because when Mrs. McConnell says Faulknerian, it sounds like she's saying *Fuck*narian. A few sleeping heads rise from their desks. A hand goes up. It's Cathi. Mrs. McConnell points to her with her chalk, "Question, Miss Serge?"

Cathi clears her throat. "I understand Faulkner was a racist, and I'm wondering why we're reading a racist book that actually uses the N-word."

"Twain, Faulkner, Welty, yep, they all used the N-word in their books. They were describing the world in which they lived. Faulkner was a diagnostician, not a fixer."

With the word fixer, again the invisible quotation marks. Cathi is not pleased with the explanation. "I don't think we should be reading a book written by a racist," she continues, her hand still half-raised in the posture of permission-seeking.

"*As I Lay Dying* is not a prescriptive on how to live one's life, Miss Serge," the teacher retorts, whirling around dramatically so that the knee-length cardigan she's wearing swirls like an umbrella caught in a gust. "Faulkner boldly unveiled the dark side of humanity, unflinchingly setting his characters in a sort of truth pudding where questions like *what is truth, what is life, what do we really want* are presented through a narrative that takes the reader to the edges of comfort. That's art, Miss Serge. Art."

In my notebook I'm working on a huge, stylized "L" which will start the word *Liar* that will cover the entire eight-by-eleven page.

Cathi says, "Still," under her breath, and the teacher continues to lecture about integrity and free will. Once it's clear that Mrs. McConnell did not, indeed, swear, heads return to desks.

In the paper today was the piece on the Greenmeadow Art Fair and Martha's smiling face above the oversized Cupworth check. Her Mt. Hood rendition, the other photo in the article. Above the fold in the Life & Lifestyles section. *Life*. Right. Cupworth's rant was also part of the article, where she said, *Art does not come cheaply, ladies and gentlemen. One must nurture the soul in order to grow one's appreciation for beauty.* The reporter left off the *bosoms on the Internet* part.

Now, the *As I Lay Dying* lesson on integrity and duplicity and truth accompanies a replay in my head of this morning's newspaper scan. No mention of me—and it made me furious with myself that I had even looked for my name or the image of my charcoaled homeless guy.

The boy next to me is still asleep. His plump brown lips are upturned, like he's dreaming something really good. Then, because we've reached the end of the period, the bell rings and he twitches like an infant, jerking his head up, wiping his mouth with the back of his arm. Desk chairs scrape the floor. Backpacks unzip, rezip. Mrs. McConnell says, "Miss Wilson, a word?"

Mrs. McConnell's hair is a gray bob which she is constantly trying to tuck behind her ears, but now, obviously flummoxed, she runs her fingertips along its part, lifting the strands up, giving her a mad scientist look. "What is going on?" she says after the last student has scurried out the door.

She's one of my favorite teachers. Like Bowerman, she's not afraid to take a stand against the administration when necessary. She's gone to bat for plenty of students for things like truancy and drinking. But she demands engagement. If you're slacking, she'll call you out on the carpet and it won't be pretty. Those kids who fell asleep in class? She'll nail them on the Faulkner exam.

"Nothing," I tell her, trying to buy time.

Her eyes lift my eyes with a mad dog laser gaze. She won't accept my answer and she'll stare me down until I give her something more. So I throw her a bone. "I've been sick."

Mrs. McConnell points to the chair next to her chair and I sit. She says, "Grief is a strange animal, Brady. It hovers and hovers and then it sees something and dives down."

That she is describing the pelicans of our Good Friday beach walk is eerie, and the chill of this creeps into my shoulders, making me spasm.

"I just want to make sure that you're taking care of yourself. Are you in counseling?"

I shrug. "We go. My parents and I. Every week since…" I can't bring myself to say *memorial service*, or even *service*.

"Family therapy is very important. But so is individual grief counseling. You need to be able to communicate freely, Brady. Do you understand what I mean?"

I nod.

"You weren't in school Friday. Were you home?"

"Yes."

"Alone?"

I nod.

Mrs. McConnell sighs. "I want you to give me your phone number. I know it's not apposite with the rules and regs, but I'm concerned." Again, her fingers make quote marks for apposite, which is a word I've never heard before. She hands me a slip of paper and pen upon which I scribble the information.

That seems to satisfy her and she tucks the slip of paper into the pocket of her long, unfashionable sweater.

*　　*　　*

Over dinner, Mom and Dad are doing the homework we're supposed to do continuously in preparation for therapy tomorrow. It's "I-statement" city while we pass the platter of turkey meatloaf and the bowl of spinach salad.

Mom: I worry that our Easter trip to the coast didn't meet with your expectations, John.

Dad: I was disappointed that we weren't able to come to an agreement about the ashes.

Mom: Brady, do you feel let down by that?

Dad: Do you, Little Bird?

Me: *shrug*.

Dad: When you don't answer us, we feel left out.

Mom: Blah, blah, I feel, blah, blah, blahblahblahblah

Finally, they get around to asking me how I felt about Martha and the Art Fair and the Cupworth Prize I didn't get. Dad has brought the offending article to the table, and he spreads it out in the space where Sabine would be sitting if she weren't dead. I'd avoided Martha all day. Didn't look at her one time during trig, ducked behind other students in the hall as she passed. On the way to art, I saw her and Nick were standing next to his locker, their fingers a feather's width from touching, so I went down the length of the middle line of the "E" and outside and back through the front door just to avoid them, knowing that now, the RIP and the kissing photo were officially stripped from the gray steel of Nick's locker. Looking at Martha's bubbly newsprint smile makes my heart and stomach collide. In a half-answer to their question, and in keeping with our "I-statement" theme, I say, "I wish I'd known. It was a little embarrassing having all of you there."

Mom says, "It was *humiliating*, and I want you to know that I've had words with Vice Principal Field about it."

"Oh, Mom, really? I don't think he knew about it. I mean, I was in his office earlier that day…"

"You were?" chimes Dad. "Why?"

"Brady has been getting into a bit of trouble," Mom offers. "At least that's what the vice principal told me. He also said that he's worried about you being in class with that boy."

"Connor?" I say, too quickly.

"Good Lord," booms Dad. "She has to sit in a classroom with that, that, jackass?"

"Now, John, no need for the name-calling."

Dad slams a fist on top of the photo of Martha and her Mt. Hood painting. "I don't want him anywhere near our family, is that understood?"

"Well, it sounds like you needn't worry. He's officially dropped out," Mom says.

My stomach and heart go another round. *Connor's dropped out?*

"Anyway, Brady, the point is, you need to let us in. You need to tell us how you feel," says my mother, mistress of duplicity.

"How I feel? You really want to know, Mom?"

"Yes, Little Bird," says Dad. "We do."

"How I feel is, I don't even know who you are anymore. Dad, you're drunk most of the time, and Mom, you sneak around like some sort of weasel." I want to mention the phone call in the beach house bathroom, but I stop myself. Dad's eyes are as bulged out as one of those pug-type dogs.

"Anger," Mom says, matter-of-factly. "Good. We can get somewhere with that."

I close my eyes thinking back on last Friday, the chain of events. The car nearly slipping down the slope. Connor, pulling it out. Getting home just in time, packing my bag for the beach, and then, spending the weekend with my empty-shell parents. Pretending that it's just another Easter weekend.

"And speaking of sneaking around," Mom adds. "Where were you Friday, when you were supposed to be in school?"

eight

Beaverton Grief & Family is wedged between a beer-making supply store and a doggy daycare in a strip mall walking distance from Greenmeadow. During our sessions, quiet pauses are often interrupted by yapping pups. On this, our fourth visit, the dogs seem especially agitated. A hound is baying and a few terrier-types are non-stop with their high-pitched barks. Mom's forehead creases with every yip. Our therapist, Dr. Stern, conducts the session calmly as ever. Leaning forward, the flesh of belly roll obscuring his belt, he invites us to "Speak our hearts."

"So, Easter marked the first family holiday without Sabine," he says, his voice slightly up-speak at the end.

"It was very difficult," says Dad. "I thought we could, you know, spread some of her ashes, have some closure, but clearly, that was premature."

Dr. Stern nods and scribbles something down in his leather diary.

Mom, fingers massaging her temples, adds, "I've heard that sometimes it takes years—a decade even—to find the right time to distribute cremains. When a child is involved."

I know part of Mom's reluctance is the Catholic thing. Nona and Nono were upset that Sabine was burned up in the first place—they had offered to pay for a burial plot. Dad refused, end of discussion. Dad says, "A decade?"

Dr. Stern directs his gaze across the room to the farthest

chair, at me. "How did it feel, Brady, at the beach without your sister?"

No hesitation, I offer, "She was there."

Dr. Stern's eyebrows go up and a series of deep growls punctuate the room. "You felt Sabine's presence then?"

"She was with us in every way."

Dad clears his throat.

"Brady has been having the hardest time letting go," Mom says. "She wore Sabine's prom dress to a school function last Thursday."

Again, eyebrows up, Dr. Stern says, "Tell us about that, Brady."

"It wasn't her *prom* dress."

Dr. Stern says, "Did you feel closer to Sabine, wearing her clothes?"

I don't offer that I hear her voice. "Sort of."

"Our daughter had a traumatic experience last week," Dad says.

"Oh?"

"I wouldn't call it traumatic. Just, well, annoying, I guess."

"Oh, come on Brady," Mom chimes, "it was horrible. She's supposed to get an award for a painting she did, and then her best friend comes in and steals her thunder. You may have seen it in yesterday's paper?"

"First of all," I say, through gritted teeth, "I wouldn't call it *horrible*. And secondly, it was a charcoal *sketch*, not a painting. And—your threatened lawsuit is the reason they gave it to Martha."

Dr. Stern says, "That must have been very difficult, Br—."

Mom interrupts, her sharp voice accompanied by a cacophony of pooches, "Lawsuit? No, it's your grades, Brady. Your truancy and insubordination. That's why they pulled the scholarship."

"Sonia," Dad says. "Please."

The ever-calm Dr. Stern raises his hands like a preacher. "One at a time, thank you. Brady, you must have felt betrayed. Tell us about that."

The word *duplicity* slithers around on my tongue like a snake. I open my mouth to let it out, the whole of it. Martha and Nick. Bowerman's spiel about the lawsuit and impropriety. Mom's secret phone call to ... who? And Connor, knowing more about Sabine than any of us. But words won't form. I just sit there dorkishly, my mouth open like a forgotten door.

Mom fills the void. "John has been drinking too much."

Dr. Stern says, "Have you had a hard time managing alcohol in the past, Mr. Wilson?"

Dad says, "For goshsakes, my daughter was just killed. A little whiskey to blunt the pain..."

"We're here, folks, as an antidote to blunting the pain. The only way out is through."

The dogs next door offer a hearty consensus.

We'd come to therapy separately, and after therapy, we trickle away from one another, three little streams branching out from the river of Grief & Family. I'm taking the bus to the library to study, I tell them. Mom gets in her Subaru, and Dad climbs into his Fusion. We agree to meet back at the house at seven.

Where I'm really going is the AT&T store, where I hope they can give me Sabine's password. It's been four days of hearing the computer voice instead of *Give me a "G"* and *Have a great day.* I want my sister's greeting back.

On the bus, bouncing down the various boulevards, passing the lingerie shops and the adult video stores with images of a bitten apple or a silhouette of a girl wearing devil horns and tail, the signs outside of these places promising to help patrons *Escape to Your Fantasy*, I remember the Johnsaffair summer—a piece of it—that I'd blocked from my mind. Sabine and I were at the beach house that July, after Mom had insisted that Dad take us out there so she could decide whether or not to divorce him. Sabine and I on the futon, Dad and Natalie in the master bedroom downstairs, Sabine said, "You know this is all Mom's fault, don't you?"

I wasn't sure what "this" referred to. We were hunkered down in a quilt, each of us reading a *Cosmo*. Sabine was glancing through an article claiming to teach women how to drive men to the brink. There was a photo of a young woman in a red bra holding a man's head just a bit away from her breasts like a bowl of steaming soup. "This" Sabine said, her index finger puncturing the pretty manicured hand of the model in the article. Then she pointed to the floor below, where our father and his mistress lay together on the waterbed Mom would ultimately replace. "That."

"Mom's fault?"

"She stopped sleeping with Dad. I know because I heard them argue about it. She complained about how much he wanted it all the time."

"Sabine, gross." I pulled the quilt up to my neck.

"Don't be a baby, Brady. You should know that men can't help themselves. It's a primordial thing. A biologic imperative. See, it says it right here in the article, 'Men will do anything for it.'"

"But we're talking about Dad, Sabine, not some dude."

"He's a boy, Brady, just like the rest of them. And now he's found himself a young girlfriend because Mom stopped putting out."

Sabine's self-assuredness, the way she slapped the *Cosmopolitan* closed and clicked off the light, leaving me with those horrific images, was so like her. I'm jerked back to the present as the bus lurches to a stop in front of BabyDoll Espresso & Girls, and the door hisses open. This is my stop.

There is a line at AT&T, so it takes me a while to get a chance to plead my case, and by the time it's my turn, I can tell the customer service representatives are exhausted. They've been screamed at all shift, putting the smiley face on for disgruntled customer after disgruntled customer. I stretch my mouth into a Sabine-sized cheering grin, and proceed to the counter, holding Sabine's cell phone out in front of me when they call, "Fifty six."

"Account number?" the clerk named Ivan asks.

"Well, I don't know it exactly. It's my parents' account."

"But they know you're here?"

"Well, it's an odd situation. My sister and I, we're on the account but..." I trail off. It's always difficult to figure out a non-shocking way to reveal Sabine's demise. The horror-struck faces, the oh-I'm-so-sorry gestures when you tell strangers that your sister was indeed the one they read about.

Ivan's face registers impatience as I stammer Dad's phone number, and finally blurt out, "She died, and I need to reset her password."

Ivan pulls out a form and hands it to me, all poker-faced. Both of our iPhones are out on the counter, Sabine's and mine. Irish twin phones like two fallen dominoes there in front of me. Ivan slaps the triplicate layers of document on the counter next to the phones. "This will need to be filled out by the account-holder. We'll need a death certificate in order to cancel the number without penalty."

"No," I say. "That's not why I'm here. We don't...at least not now...we don't want to cancel the number. I just want access to the voicemail."

Ivan sighs. "You're not authorized, is the problem. We have a non-authorized minor sitch here. You'll need your parents to call in."

I want to jump over the counter and bash Ivan's head against the computer monitor he's staring into, his smug, cold eyes reviewing the facts and digits and codes that make up the Wilson account. I want to shake some humanness into his geeky, lifeless expression. *She's dead.* I want to shout. *Dead. And you're talking about procedure?*

Instead, I take the form and fold it up and put it in the pocket of my windbreaker, and cram the phones in with it. "Thanks, anyway," I manage, before pivoting away so the next disgruntled customer can have it out with Ivan.

Outside, as I walk by BabyDoll Espresso & Girls, I try really hard to hold back the tears that are stinging the gooey parts of my eyes. Ever since the accident, it seems that there's been nothing but big boulders in my way. Boulders the size of the ones in front of Jesus' tomb, where he went before he "rose again according to the scripture." I think some more about the resurrection story. The part of the creed that goes "He will come again in glory to judge the living and the dead."

Sabine and I, when we attended mass with Nona, we'd mumble right along, all the words glued together in one long mush: We believe in the Holy Spirit, the Lord, the giver of Life blahblahblahblah until, We look for the resurrection of the dead and life of the world to come. Amen.

Back on the bus, I find myself mouthing the last part, my words barely a whisper. *We look for the resurrection of the dead and life of the world to come.* My sister in limbo and her greeting in limbo with her. I know what I have to do. I have to free her greeting. I have to hear her voice again. I can't allow her to die, to truly die, this way.

On my own phone, I bring up Facebook. The *Beenick*

Page and its cartoon lilies and sad emoticons are gone. Just like that. Sabine's Facebook is still there though. Her timeline cover photo, taken a week before she died, her squad lined up. And in the middle, there's Connor, holding her one foot, like the prince in Cinderella, as she performs her infamous single-leg scorpion, one leg bent impossibly behind her, reaching the spot between her shoulders. Her back is curved like a Grecian urn. Her bare stomach arched. The way his hands are wrapped around her base instep, those muscled wrestling arms, his eyes glued to her leg, like it's a precious jewel—there's no way he would have harmed her. I know right then, there's just no way.

I don't think it through too hard when I do it. I just run my fingers over the touchpad of my iPhone and press send. And by the time the bus pulls up to the stop near my house, my phone responds. YES says the message. I CAN DO THAT. NOW? WHERE?

nine

Connor meets me at the edge of Forest Park, on a trail known for the disposal of dead prostitutes. Amid newly fronded ferns and tri-petaled, pale purple trillium, he greets me with a slouched posture, again shrouded in a hoodie, but this time without my sister's earring dangling from his lobe. "Hey," he says.

"So," I say. "I heard you quit school."

"Yeah? Well, I'm thinking of transferring to BALC, finish up there."

Beaverton Alternative Learning Center or *balk*, as it's sometimes called, is the school where the druggies go before flunking out completely. I must be wincing because Connor follows it up with, "No, seriously, they have a great wrestling team."

"You're going to go back to wrestling, then?"

Connor slouches further into himself and says, "I think my cheer career is like, you know, over."

My fingers are playing with the phones in my pocket. I want to get on with it. I'll barely get home by 7:00 as it is. "So, thanks for, uh, meeting me. You think you can help?"

"Jailbreak Sabine's phone? Yeah, I can do that. But I'm not sure it's a good idea."

The boulder of Ivan's unhelpfulness appears in Connor's face. Not him, too.

"I mean, why?" he asks. "Why do you want to get into

her business?"

"Personal reasons," I say.

"Look, I know you two were tight, but there's stuff about her you don't know and, well, I don't think she would want you messing around there."

"Like what?"

"Brady, you should let this go."

An unleashed dog comes romping up and sniffs our crotches, its frantic owner behind it, calling "Cookie. Cookie. Get over here."

"Let *what* go? What are you getting at?"

Connor holds the runaway dog's collar while the owner fumbles up the trail. Whatever Connor's referring to will have to wait until we're done with this interruption. I'm impatient. I should be getting home. My fingers shuffle the two phones in my pocket.

Once the owner and his pet are out of earshot Connor says, "How well do you know Nick?"

"He practically lived at our house the last couple of years. Pretty good, I guess. Where are you going with this?"

"Sabine had some secrets," Connor says. "I made a promise to her. She told me stuff in confidence."

"Oh for fuck's sake." I'm furious now. Why would Sabine confide in Connor and not me? "Look," I tell him. "I just want to hear her voice. I miss it. Can you do that? Just clear her voicemail so I can hear her again?" I pull Sabine's phone out and hand it over, like it's a foreign document and Connor's the translator.

Connor takes the phone, puts it in his pocket and we walk along the darkening path up and up, when we should be walking down, back toward our respective homes. It's getting chillier and my windbreaker isn't enough. An early evening breeze shoots through to my bones. A couple of birds, big black ones, flap the air as they cut across the path in front of us. Into the silence between us Connor says, "That so-called boyfriend of hers, he's an asshole."

"You keep saying that. I mean, I know you guys had your differences, but he really loved my sister."

Connor lets out the sort of laugh that's not really a laugh. A sneer mixed with disbelief. "Love. Right. Who he loves is himself. The guy's up for 6A lacrosse player of the year. He's got full ride offers all over the country. Kid just turned eighteen, can barely vote, and he acts like he's Bill Fucking Gates."

"Bill Gates?"

"OK, maybe David Beckham. Thinks he walks on water. If I told you what I know about him? Jesus."

Something occurs to me. "So, was he dating Martha before Sabine died?"

Connor shakes his head. "Nah. He was obsessed with your sister. And not in a good way."

We get to a fork, and we follow the sign for Wildwood, going deeper into the woods. It's past the time when the runners are out. The dog-walkers are all home. It's getting colder and darker. I don't feel scared though. Next to Connor, weirdly, I feel safer than I've felt in weeks. "Spill it."

"Nick? Let's just say, the *Beenick* thing? You know, all that Brangelina stuff? Bullshit."

We hike through muddy ruts, our sneakered feet in step. Where it's really mucky there are planks. The path wanders up and down. The creek below us flows in its spring enthusiasm. A few bold crickets chirp. Or maybe they're frogs. Night sounds are overtaking day sounds and we're continuing on.

A question pops out of me, so fast that it doesn't even register until it's out of my mouth, "Did *you* love her?"

"Your sister? Shit. Everyone did. She's, she *was*, the hottest girl at Greenmeadow."

His answer feels like a line from *Cosmo*, and it disappoints me. The dismissiveness of it. I slap his arm, lightly, like you do with a good friend who's just pissed you off. Then, "I was looking at her timeline picture. Her doing that Scorpion stunt, and you holding onto her foot that way? That looked real to me, the way you held her."

"That Scorpion stunt. Yeah. There was no holding your sister. Put it that way."

He stops on the trail, fishes around his jeans pocket, and pulls out a doob, then a match. Lights it, cups his hand and sucks in the skunky weed and the tip of it lights up his face. Around the joint in his mouth he says, "Don't imagine you want a hit?"

I shake my head. "I need to get back."

We turn around and retrace our steps, the marijuana cigarette lighting our way. When we're close to the main road, I change my mind about the messages. "Look, I want to know. I need to know. If there is stuff on her phone, don't erase it."

"You're aiding and abetting a criminal, Brady," he says. "I think it's illegal to break into someone's privacy."

"You *did* love her, didn't you?"

Connor sucks in another hit. Doesn't answer. Even though it's totally dark now, I have the sense that all around us are living things. Crickets, crows, ivy.

We part ways and agree to meet the following day. It's nearly 8:00 by the time I board the bus. When I finally see our porch light illuminating the driveway, and pad up toward the front door, I stop in my tracks beside Sabine's Volvo. The barely shining map light is on, and there's Dad, reclined in the driver's seat, his eyes closed. In his fist is a bottle of something, and next to him, on the passenger's seat, is the Ziploc baggie we'd brought to the coast, filled with the charred bits and fragments of his oldest daughter.

ten

Bowerman keeps me after class. This is starting to be a "thing," this, let's check in with the grieving girl and make sure she's not self-harming. Seriously, I see them scanning my forearms, these teachers. I know they're worried, but all of their scrutinizing makes me feel itchy.

She doesn't scan me though, Bowerman. After the other students leave and she closes the door, she talks fast. "Mrs. Cupworth would like you, *us*, to visit with her this afternoon. Are you up for it?"

I think about my plan to meet Connor, but that's not until later. "Cupworth? Why?"

"She smelled a rat that night, and she wants more information. You game?"

I'm intrigued, I admit, but I've let the whole Art Fair debacle go. I really don't feel like revisiting the humiliation of last week. "I don't know, Ms. Bowerman. I mean, what's done is done."

Bowerman grips my arms and looks me square, "Brady, that's just it, it's not done. Mrs. Cupworth loved your sketch. In fact, she bought it that night. She was disappointed with the decision to give the scholarship to Martha. When she heard about the extenuating circumstances surrounding your grades, she even said, 'The child just lost a sibling, have a heart.'"

"Well, there's always next year, right?"

Bowerman lets go of my arms, and her voice takes on a

pleading tone. "Just come with me. She wants to meet you. She thinks, as do I, that you're incredibly talented."

Painting, sketching, it's all fallen so far to the back burner. All I want to do is listen to Sabine's voice. Listen to the messages on her phone. Find out what was really going on with her the day she died. But I nod anyway. Take the slip of paper Bowerman hands me. The address is another West Hills mansion. This one high up on Vista, above the jumper bridge, where Portland's most devastated commit suicide year after year. "I have to be somewhere right after that, though. I hope she won't think me rude if I just stay for a few minutes."

"I'm sure that will be fine. Let's hear what she has to say."

At lunch, Martha flags me down. It's out now, her relationship with Nick, and they're inseparable. Helping each other through grief. They've managed to position themselves as virtuous. *Elegiac*, is what Mrs. McConnell might call it. They are soldiering forth, the way Sabine would have wanted. Her periodic best friend and her boyfriend aligned to honor her memory throughout time. Seeing them in the hall, holding hands, is like being pushed down on a bed of rusty nails.

"Brady, wait up." she sings. Her boyfriend chorusing the notion.

"I need to get a bagel," I say, and continue on down the hall to the student store—a retail establishment set up in an abandoned classroom, manned by Marketing for the Real World students. It's a gut class, one you take for a guaranteed "A."

"Mind if we join you?" says Martha.

I do, but I shrug.

Nick sidles up next to me, the Axe smell of him. "How you doin'?"

"Not great."

"How's the fam?"

By *fam*, I assume he means my parents. "As bad as can be expected," I say.

"Yeah, well, I miss her too."

Martha wedges in between us as we round the corner to the store, possessively taking Nick's hand. "We haven't seen you around at all the usual places, Brady. It's like, you've just disappeared. People ask about you, you know."

I want to change the subject. I haven't been eating lunch with my usual group—the art kids and the brainiacs. I haven't returned phone calls and texts, and I don't "like" stuff on Facebook every other minute, so I suppose that's cause for concern. It's just, I really don't know how to be me again. When your sister is the most popular girl in school, you've got a role. Now? I have no idea what my role is. Clearly, I'm not an "outstanding art student" anymore. Partially, thanks to Martha.

"I hear you might go to Penn State next year," I manage, underlining the notion that soon, Nick will be moving on to the next thing, and Martha will be here, at Greenmeadow, alone.

"Might actually be staying in town. UP just offered."

Of course. And the fact that Martha's family is one of the campus's major donors had nothing to do with that. The smell of rats abounds around here.

"We're hoping to keep this guy in the home town, you know?" says Martha, all smiles.

"Nice," I say. "OK, I'm going to get some lunch now. See you later."

"Brady," Martha says. "Are you mad at me?"

I stare at the incredulity of her remark. I'm thinking *Fuck*nerian thoughts. Duplicity. Falsehoods. Back-stabbing. "Mad? Oh, Martha, that doesn't even approach how I feel about you. And him.'"

Martha truly looks hurt, but I don't care. And Nick? *You deserve each other*, I think.

The two lovebirds stand there, holding hands in the hall, their stunned and stupid faces all plastered with concern. Then, I swirl away from them and march through the door to the Marketing for the Real World store to buy a stale pumpernickel bagel.

Lilith Cupworth's mansion sits above the road at the end of a steep, curving drive. I walk up its smooth surface, noting the bank of lilies of the valley that grace the borders. Rhodies are blooming behind the flowers, and beyond that are trees from the historic register. An enormous Doug fir and a redwood and the hugest Ponderosa in Portland, all stamped with greenish copper plaques. This house once belonged to one of Portland's founding lumbermen. All the fortunes in this town came from trees. I think about the Garden of Eden. The serpent. The apple tree. That ponderosa, I'd love to slap that on canvas. Maybe paint a heroin addict lying against it. A nice juxtaposition. I don't know why these things occur to me so frequently. The majestic and the decrepit side-by-side.

The Cupworth House is grander than anything I've ever seen. The main building is brick, with a portico on one side. Ivy growing up and over the roof. The opposite side of the house is a sun porch with hundreds of tiny windows in a checkerboard pattern of clear and stained glass. Two thick vines of wisteria snake up from either end, coming together in the middle like the fingers on Michelangelo's Hands of God.

I see Bowerman's Camry parked next to some fancy foreign car. The brass knocker on the door is a ring in a lion's mouth. It's ice cold when I grab it, and I knock quickly and let it go. I expect a butler to answer, or one of those classically appointed French maids. It's Mrs. Cupworth herself though, as the heavy door peels open. The outspoken dowager invites me into the foyer, and extends her smooth, manicured hand. "So good to finally meet you," she says.

"Pleased," I say, in that faux British tone I've seen a zillion times in the movies.

Bowerman has traded her usual Oregon Country Fair look for a blazer and pantsuit. Her dreads are roped back, in something approaching a chignon. She stands next to Lilith Cupworth conspiratorially, like I've interrupted a BFF session.

"Come," says Cupworth, gesturing to that fantastic glass porch which, it turns out is called a *conservatory*. "I've made lemonade."

Lilith Cupworth is dressed to the nines, as they say. Skirt, blouse, stockings, a full face. Her hair is what you talk about when you talk about blue haired old ladies. Her posture is ballerina perfect. I feel like a complete slouch in my usual tee-shirt dress, leggings and Keds outfit. She pours fresh-squeezed lemonade into the crystal goblet in front of me and offers an array of treats on a three-tiered platter. I put a linen napkin on my lap, but don't reach for the pink macaroons that beckon, lest I get crumbs all over the perfect tea party setting.

"Mrs. Bowerman tells me you've applied to the San Francisco Art Institute?"

The lemonade is sour, and my mouth puckers around my answer, "The pre-college summer program. Yes. But that was before…"

Mrs. Cupworth leans toward me, "Before your sister passed. And let me say how sorry I am for your loss, dear."

"Thanks. Thank you. I'm not sure whether I can go. This year."

"Brady would be a shoe-in," Bowerman adds. "But, the

timing might not be right."

It's then that I notice my drawing, set up on an easel at the edge of the conservatory. She's put it in a sleek black frame, matted in gold. It looks real. Like art. She sees me gazing at it. "I was obviously quite taken with it, Brady. The eye you have. It really made me wonder what you could do with proper tools. Heavier paper? Maybe a Ritmo-type pencil?"

I glance around the room. Martha's Mt. Hood is nowhere to be seen, and I feel bad that I'm pleased about that.

"Your teacher tells me that you're quite an advocate. You've shared your thoughts on art education in the school paper?"

"I was interviewed once. But nothing I said was as, you know, articulate, as the speech you gave the other night. That was great what you said about being doomed if we cut art from the schools." I'm aware that I sound like a complete idiot. I take another sip of lemonade just so I'll stop embarrassing myself.

"Yes, well, I'll cut to the chase here. Mrs. Bowerman let me in on the, well, circumstances regarding the rescinding of the scholarship, and I have to say, that sort of political ballyhoo is exactly what gets my dander up. I do not like being made a fool of, Brady, so, I thought I would bring you here to, well, prepare you, I suppose."

"Prepare me?"

"I'm going to make a bit of a stink. I'm due for one."

A nastily happy thought occurs to me then. "Are you going to make Martha forfeit the prize?" I'm mortified, actually, at the lilt in my voice, the enthusiasm, as the words clatter out of me.

Bowerman intervenes. "No, Brady, that would be awkward. But, we are planning on calling up that reporter and setting her straight. We'd like to propose they do a feature on the vanishing funding for arts in the schools."

Mrs. Cupworth starts talking before Bowerman's even

closed her mouth. It feels like they're my parents, finishing each other's sentences. Rehearsed co-conspirators. The dowager is excited, her cheeks are flushed, and one strand of her bluish coif has loosed over a penciled brow, "And, we feel that the school made you ineligible for the scholarship for self-serving reasons, Brady. You deserved to win that prize. And, in fact, I am planning to match the check. I would enjoy helping you explore the edges of your talent and passion for the visual arts, young lady. I'd like to explore a patronage, a place for you to sketch and paint as time allows."

I really don't know what to say. The generosity and enthusiasm of these two women is overwhelming. For a whole minute, I forget about Sabine and meeting up with Connor. I forget about the various sadnesses and betrayals, and a genuine joy seeps into the place under my ribs. Despite the cold, sour lemonade, I'm all warm inside.

And then my pocket buzzes with the announcement of an incoming text. I glance down and see that it's Martha. She wants to talk. She didn't like the way we left things. Just like that, the happy feeling drains away. It's past 4:00. I'm supposed to meet Connor in half an hour. I look up and across the table at my host and my advocate, hoping that my face looks less anxious than I feel. I smile. "Mrs. Cupworth, Mrs. Bowerman, thank you. Thank you for your kindness. Both of you. I'd love to talk more about art and your thoughts, but I have some, um, urgent family things to attend to."

Mrs. Cupworth takes in a breath, and then stands. She takes both my hands in hers, the way older, proper people do, and she says, "Dear, I'd like to continue this conversation when you have more time. Perhaps you could come again?"

The wisteria scratches the glass outside as the afternoon breeze picks up. "I'd love to," I say, before slipping out of the mansion and down to the roads where the normal people live.

eleven

All the way down Vista, past the suicide bridge—where they just this week installed 9-foot screens to deter jumpers—past two Starbucks, and into the neighborhood that will lead to the park and then to Connor and whatever he's found on Sabine's phone, Martha's texts intrudes.

We really need 2 talk.

Can u meet me at Sbux?

I hate that u r mad at me.

I'm mad at myself for even looking at them. Martha's total OCD behavior when someone's mad at her is endearing, in a way, but I really want to stay mad. How can she just charge forward with her life the way she has after Sabine's death? And as for Nick? Was his Versace-slash-Johnny-Cash-Black grief just an act?

The week after my sister died, Nick was glued to our house. We were all zombies, sitting around the kitchen table, writing Sabine's obituary. Deciding what picture to put in the paper. Where to have the big gathering after the funeral, whether to call it "a celebration of life" or "a memorial service." It was like putting on some theater production with a week to cast the show, write it, rehearse our lines, decide on a venue and print out the tickets. All the while struggling in the numbness and disbelief that we'd lost Sabine.

We needed Nick for so many things. The Greenmeadow choir sang at her funeral, and Nick arranged that. He got the graphic design department at school to create the programs. And then there were the bread-and-butter details. Stuff like, *In lieu of flowers, please send remembrances to The Humane Society.* Martha came up with that—even though we weren't exactly known for being one of those *dog* families. Why not cancer? I wondered. Why not the environment? Or even arts education? Naturally, I could see why we didn't choose the cheerleading squad.

"When a child dies, it's customary to choose an animal-related charity," Martha assured us. And Martha would know that sort of stuff, so The Humane Society it was.

Ironically, I'm pretty sure that was the beginning of Nick and Martha's romance. And it happened under our roof, poring over the details of Sabine's send-off. Nick helped with errands around town, and Martha coordinated casseroles. They both brainstormed the death announcement with Mom and ran interference when reporters wanted to talk with us. And then Martha color-coded all of my sister's clothes, tidied up her room—staging it as though it were for sale. She created "the museum of Sabine," explaining that she wanted to spare us the pain of having to sift through Sabine's things until we were ready, but when we *were* ready, she explained, it would be easier to deal with an orderly version of her life.

At first, I was grateful for their company. Dad was a mess. Not sleeping, not really awake. He sat in the family room in front of the flat screen for hours in a half-conscious state. A bottle of Jameson's by his side. Mom, meanwhile, was an animated robot. Like some alien creature had inhabited her body, she was constantly moving from one thing to the next, check-off lists in hand. It was only after the service that she started to sputter and falter—forgetting to turn off burners, leaving her phone at home while slipping the remote to the TV in her purse. Having Nick see all of this, be around it, began to feel weird. His presence—the perfect 18-yr-old boy with everything to live for, everything ahead of him—began to remind me in deep, ugly ways that my sister would never grow any older. Soon, I would be the older sister. I would be a senior, then a high school graduate. College, career, marriage, kids, middle age, on and on I'd continue, and Sabine would always be eighteen. "They were so in love," Mom exclaimed, wistfully, evening after evening, thumbing through the Spring Fling photos Martha had already glued into an album.

I began to resent that Nick and Martha would just show up at our house. They wouldn't even knock half the time, just show up, bearing bereavement cards and flowers and poems. Whole classes had created science fair-type triptych boards of scribbled condolences. Our living room was a roadside death remembrance, with stuffed animals and mass candles and the occasional brass crucifix spread out in front of our fireplace. When more sympathy swag came Mom was always, "so touched," and Dad, well, he'd just nod and grunt. Occasionally lift one of these well-wishings up to his nose and sniff it. As if there was a way to evoke Sabine from the odor of a dried herb garland.

Finally, I realized it was up to me to stop the madness. I asked Martha to back off. Nicely, but firmly. And Nick, well, he got the message too when I asked him to haul all the stuff to our storage unit. "Mom and Dad, they need a break from it," I told him, and handed him the key to our 10-by-10 foot space at SelfStor along with Mom's Subaru fob.

So Nick moved on. The most popular girl at school had died tragically, and her lover's stock soared. Nick was surrounded by groupies and mourners—an entourage of sobbing teenagers following him around. Connor, the killer, meanwhile, went from being a fairly popular kid to the bearer of the plague. And one day, they had it out.

I was AWOL when it happened, so everything I know,

I heard from Martha and other gossips, like Cathi Serge. Apparently, Connor just walked up to Nick, right there in the hall, amid the black balloons and the hankies and the plastic flowers and the magnetic RIP, and balled up his meaty fist—the same hand that held and then failed to hold my sister as she flipped and stretched and leapt through the air. Connor shoved that fist into Nick's perfect jaw.

It was ugly. They went at it like fighting dogs, rolling around on the floor of the spine of Greenmeadow's "E." Fists and flesh and then some blood. Girl screams, and teachers trying to break them apart. A big assembly afterwards where grief counselors were called in. What a mess. And now Connor has dropped out, and Nick's dating Martha.

Martha. More texts bleeping into my phone.

We're not the bad guys.

Brady? Is this thing on?

So I cave. Text back.

I'm in NW. Dragonfly Coffee House? 4:30?

B thr soon as I can, she messages.

Connor will have to wait. I text him that I'm running late. *NP* is what I get back. Stoner boy shorthand for *whatever*.

I order a double chai with almond milk and a lemon poppy seed scone, and take a seat on a puffy velvet pillow under one of the café's jeweled chandeliers. After Cupworth's porch, the Victorian feel of the Dragonfly is perfect. I conjure some grace and poise, channeling Lilith and her manners and elegance. I cross my legs at the knee and sip the foam off my drink without slurping. I will be gracious to Martha. I will rise above my anger and hurt. I will.

By the time she finally plows through the door, it's well after 5:00 and I'm finished with my drink, picking the last poppy seeds from the napkin, licking them off my index finger in very un-Cupworth style. Martha comes over and wraps her arms around the side of me, as though my decision to meet and talk means all is forgiven. She says, "Sorry to keep you. The buses, they're so slow."

"What about your car?" I ask.

She looks sheepishly down at the floor. "Nick's borrowing it. You know, he doesn't have a car, and, well, he has so much going on."

"Oh."

"He doesn't know I'm meeting you. Just, FYI."

I raise a brow.

"I mean, not that he has anything to say about it? It's just, you know, complicated with us."

Martha goes up to the counter for her coffee, and I'm still not sure what I will or won't tell her. Part of me wants to let her know about Connor, that I've asked him to unlock Sabine's phone, but then I know it'll get back to Nick, and she's right, everything now is so complicated. By the time she returns, I've decided to keep mum about Connor, but let her know about Cupworth.

Martha reaches into her purse and pulls out a little pill box, then washes her medication down with a swig of coffee. Martha's always taking a "little something" for nerves.

"It must be strange for you to see the two of us together," she starts in, with a clearly practiced speech. "So soon after the accident."

I put a hand up to stop her. "Martha, it's your life. His life. None of my business."

"Then, what's the deal? Is this about the Art Fair? Because if it is…"

"It's not. I mean, it was. A little. But that's working itself out."

Martha, her healthy mahogany hair and her steaming black coffee sit across from me. A round metal table in between us. "How so?"

"Mrs. Cupworth, apparently she likes my drawing. I was just over there. She's, well, she and Bowerman are planning on going public with the politics behind the prize."

Martha looks as though she's just watched someone get stabbed in the street. Her eyes all Anime she says, "What do you mean, *politics*?"

"Why they gave the award to you and not me. Don't worry. They assured me that they're not taking your prize back."

"Well, Brady, student-in-good-standing was a requirement. And, you haven't really been pulling the grades lately."

The way she's arguing with me, her finger practically wagging in my face, like a teacher or a parent, it's just plain weird. I want to say more about it, but instead, I scan my napkin for more poppy seeds, and stick my seed-speckled finger in my mouth.

"So, what are they planning on doing? On saying?"

I shrug. "Never mind. Forget I said anything. You're right. I'm a loser, I didn't deserve to win, end of story."

Martha reaches her olive branch hand out close to my gooey finger, but I don't grasp it. "Oh Brady, I'm sorry. Clearly, I'm being insensitive. Here's the thing. I'm up for Rose Festival, you know? And, being a junior and all, it's unlikely they'll choose me, but it would look so good on my transcripts. I was able to add the thing about winning the Cupworth, and it's quite a coup. It would just be sort of embarrassing if something came out that I won it by default."

When Martha says default, she emphasizes the *de* instead of the *fault*, and the word is as wrong to my ear as it is to my heart. She really thinks her Mt. Hood was best-in-show? "I'm sure it won't factor in. Princess Martha."

"*Queen* Martha," she counters, putting an invisible tiara

on her glossy Covergirl head. She'd be perfect as Rose Festival Queen. I can see her waving to the masses from the seat of the big fat float, a white-gloved Rosarian at the wheel, shepherding her through the streets of her Fair City.

My phone makes the text-message noise and ever-attentive Martha chimes, "Your parents wondering when you're coming home? Want to ride the bus back with me?"

It's Connor with a, *wassup?*

"Uh, yeah, well, I have a couple more errands to run. Library and whatnot. Maybe we can get together over the weekend or something."

"That would be fantastic. But Brady, you're sure we're good? Solid?"

I nod my affirmation. We're as solid as we ever were I guess. Which has always seemed a little more on Martha's terms than mine.

Connor's waiting for me at the Witch's House—the unofficial party spot a mile or so up the trail coming out of Lower Macleay Park. It's where Nick and Sabine first "did it," Sabine told me. Nick had a backpack full of supplies: a blanket, some pills to "relax" her. "I was super nervous," she'd told me the next day. "The pills—they helped loosen me up."

I'd wanted to hear everything. What it felt like, what Nick said to her during their love-making, but Sabine just waved me off with a, "I'm glad I got that out of the way."

When I finally get to the stone ruin Connor's behind a jagged pillar, leaned up against a tree, a bear scratching its hide. His usual hoodie hugs his broad shoulders; his legs are bare from the knees, muscled legs half-covered with cargo shorts. A Portland Timbers cap sits backwards on his head, and Sabine's earring dangles and sparkles, dancing in the waning afternoon rays.

"Let's bounce," he says, his chin pointing up-trail to a uniformed somebody in a Day-Glo pinnie who seems to be eyeing us.

We walk up toward the upper parking lot, and I'm already regretting my choice of footwear—a sort of rubber soled bedroom slipper with no arch support. Hill-walking seems to be the theme today. I can tell Connor's a little annoyed that I'm not keeping pace.

"So, what was the hold up?" he asks after we're out of earshot of the pinnie police.

I'm not sure how to answer that, exactly, so I just say. "School stuff."

Connor's not buying it. "Anyone know about, um, that you're here? With me?"

"You sound really creepy now. Like, are you planning on slashing my throat and throwing me in the ivy with all the dead prostitutes?" I'm kidding, of course, but Connor gives me a *really?* look.

We keep walking, and the suspense is beginning to kill me. But, I figure, let him spill it in his own time, whatever he found out jailbreaking Sabine's phone, it's got to be big, the way he keeps walking without talking. We're winding up the hairpins, and Connor won't stop checking over his shoulder. We're close to the Audubon crossing, it's not getting any earlier, and my feet are beginning to sting. Finally, I can't hold it in anymore. "C'mon, Connor, what the hell?"

He stops and points to a small clearing where the oaks haven't leafed out yet, and I follow him off the trail. The hair on Connor's calves is dark blond, and there's a lot of it. His green eyes and their flecks of amber. Those lips. He says, "I figured out her password."

"Seriously?"

"Wasn't that hard, Brady."

"Well, I tried her birthday and Nick's birthday …"

"Yeah, well you forgot one."

"Huh?"

Connor dots the middle of my forehead with his index finger.

"No way."

"Way."

"How do you know *my* birthday?"

"Um, Facebook? You're pretty dumb for a smart chick."

"Did you save the messages? Were there a lot of them?" I'm shocked at how happy I am, just anticipating hearing the sound of my sister's voice again.

"You'll have to delete a few of them. She's at the capacity."

I hold out my palm, expecting Connor to fork it over, but he just crams his hands into the pockets of his shorts.

"What."

"Brady. I'm not so sure you want to hear what's on her phone."

"Oh, come on. Some bullshit sexy talk from that bonehead formerly known as her boyfriend. I can take it."

"It's not that. Look. Sit down." Connor points to a rotted log.

I keep standing. "What's the big mystery?"

He sighs and looks off in the middle distance, like people do when they're searching for the right words. "Sabine told me some stuff, you know, in the weeks before that day."

"Like what?"

"Like … oh, man. This is hard."

"Stop it Connor. C'mon it's getting late."

"She, well, she was in trouble."

"What kind of trouble?" I'm thinking, maybe she got caught cheating on a test? Or maybe there's some MIP thing we never knew about. "I mean, it's no secret she liked to party."

"Your sister was, um, she was pregnant."

The words *sister* and *pregnant*, so weird side-by-side that way. Sabine was on the pill. I thought. "Really? But …"

"Well, here's the thing. I knew she suspected she was knocked up, but she didn't know, or she told me she didn't know for sure. But the thing is, Nick? Well he was on her case about gaining weight. She went off the pill because she thought it was making her fat."

I sit down on the mossy log now, my head and my feet are both pounding. Connor reaches into his pocket and pulls out Sabine's purple-covered phone. "On the voicemail, apparently she had an appointment to, you know, abort it. They were calling to confirm. But that's not really the worst."

I'm still in shock over hearing Sabine was pregnant. "What do you mean, 'the worst'?"

Connor gazes down at the Forest. He's not looking at me when he says, "Nick, he threatened her. A lot."

"*Threatened* her?"

Connor shakes his head. "He's such an asshole."

I stand up and grab the phone from him, punch in my birthdate, and listen to Nick call my sister the worst names imaginable. He tells her she's cheap. That she is trying to trap him. That she's ruining his life. That he's not even sure it's *his*. One horrible, horrible message where he says, *You're a skanky little whore. If you're pregnant, there's no knowing who the father is.* And, *All you are is a trashy little social climber. You come from nothing, and you'll end up with nothing.*

All of this, days before he shows up at our house in tears, pledging undying love, falling apart on our front stoop, overtaken by grief.

My face must be turning colors, because Connor says, "Wow, Brady, you OK?"

I close my eyes, anger charging through me like steam in a teakettle. I hold the phone in the air, the offending instrument. "Connor, what the hell? I mean, if I let Mom and Dad know about Sabine, it'll really crush them. But I want them to hear this. I want them to know what kind of a shit Nick is. I want everyone to know."

Connor nods. Looks down. "Yeah."

And then it hits me. The pieces come together. "You didn't drop her. She passed out. From the pregnancy. She fainted. Oh, Connor, we have to let people know."

"She was a little woozy, but that's not what happened. Your sister? She was so competitive. It wasn't enough to do one flip, she had to do two. I told her not to, I told her, especially with the way she was feeling, but she had to prove something. Especially to that Dickwad."

I close my eyes and see her up on top of the world, before she fell. It was a preview of their routine for State. It all comes clear. Sabine wanted to win it for them, the second year in a row. But I didn't know. Nobody knew that she was planning to do an extra flip. Right before she fell, everyone's phones up in the air to capture it, a zillion iPhones poised, and Sabine, imagining herself going viral, flying and spinning and tucking. Her athletic, amazing body, hurling itself through the air on the way to Connor's arms. Instead, she became the cheerleader who broke her neck.

And me, in La La Land, gazing off at something else entirely. Why wasn't I watching her when it happened? Why didn't I try and stop her?

Connor sighs. "I still fucked up, Brady. I should have moved three more inches. I would have caught her then."

It's so easy to find the right words to comfort Connor. Much easier than to forgive myself. "It wasn't your fault. It wasn't. That extra flip, the way she always had something to prove. To her. To Nick. To the world."

Connor shrugs. The earring glints in the dying light. Another evening in the woods with this boy. I don't think about it, just reach out and touch the little jewel coming off Connor's lobe, like a little kid in a gift shop grabbing stuff they're not supposed to. My fingers brush his chin and there's just the tiniest sandpaperiness there. A jolt of something hits me in the gut. It makes me nervous, and I'm not sure why. "I've got to go," I tell him, and we start walking back down the trail.

twelve

We walk back down the trail, past the Witch's House where there are no park ranger types, no people of any sort. Balch Creek is flowing hard just below us, but we can't see it, as dusk has settled, and any daylight left is just what reflects off of some white granite boulders. The water rush sound accompanies us back to civilization. My feet hurt a lot now, but I have to stride big to keep up with Connor; we need to get out of the forest before it's pitch black.

He still has a little deodorant smell, but now it's mixed with a spring soil scent. Our shoulders are nearly touching. I'm aware of how close my hip is to his hip. The jelly feeling in my gut is both lower and higher now—traveling like water on tissue. We haven't spoken a word to each other since leaving the clearing. Finally, house lights glow ahead of us. He says, "My parents are pretty close to sending me away."

My ears lock down on those words, my throat closes around them. I'm aware of sweat, suddenly, little dots of it at my temples, on my palms. A heartbeat tries pumping blood around, as though I'm a deer in a fight-or-flight stance. "Why?"

Stupid question, I know, but it's all that manages to come out of my closed-up throat.

"It's the classic stepfather scene. All he needed was one more reason to hate my guts. My dad lives over in Bend, they want to send me there."

"But I thought," I stammer, "you were going to BALC?"

"Yeah, well, guess not."

In the rising moonlight, the shadows on Connor's face make a jigsaw line from his forehead to chin. I want to capture it so bad that I can almost feel the shape of a charcoal stick in my hand, a blurred edge of gray on canvas. Again, Sabine's earring, the silver of it, catches white light. I swallow, and have to hold myself back from running my fingers up and down the length of his face. It's that beautiful.

"When?" I manage, my question a whisper.

"Soon, maybe. I'm looking for a construction job or something. Digging ditches, whatever. I'll be eighteen in a few months, if I had money saved up, I could live on my own. Or travel, you know?"

That Connor Christopher really believes this makes me want to hug him. "Connor, I think we need to set the record straight. About the accident. Your parents, the school, they'd reconsider."

Connor shakes his head. "Here's the thing. I've got my whole life ahead of me. I can live it any way I want. Sabine doesn't have those options."

I think of the Classics in Context class, Mrs. McConnell and her duplicity versus integrity lecture. "That's very Faulknerian of you," I tell Connor.

He stares at me like I've lost my mind. "You're such a nerd, Brady. You're like the opposite of your sister."

That should hurt my feelings, what he just said, but it doesn't. Being around Connor makes me feel *real*er, somehow. There's some sort of truth serum thing happening to me, and I'm not afraid. Of anything. I say, "Sabine and me, we're Irish twins, you know."

"I don't know what that means, but I do know that Sabine thought you were wicked smart. Like, over the top."

"She said that?"

"All the time," Connor says, grinning. And I notice for the first time, there's a dimple on the earring side of his face.

"She talks to me," he says.

This is uncanny; I want more. "Like, what do you mean? Has conversations with you—from the great beyond?"

"Not lately. But until about a week ago, it was like she would guide me. I'd hear her voice talking me in or out of things."

We're almost at the bus stop now, and I start to feel panicky. I want to keep talking to Connor Christopher. "Connor..." I say, standing stock still right there on the sidewalk.

The way he looks at me when I say his name, it's like Sabine's inside him. For a tiny second, I really believe that she is. "Same," is all I can manage to say.

I see the 15 bus chugging toward us. "You gonna get on?" I ask.

"Nah. I'm gonna keep walking. I'm in no hurry to get back to it. My folks are like so shitty right now, it's best I get home after they've gone to bed."

I nod, but I'm sad. If I weren't already way late and my feet weren't killing me, I'd walk over the hill with him. It's a good six or seven miles though, so I wave goodbye like a kindergarten kid getting on a school bus. And I'm not even embarrassed by my dorkiness.

My cell phone has eight voicemails on it. Dad, Martha, Mom, Mom, Martha. A few from some kids in my art class. On the bus toward downtown I delete them all without listening. I'm feeling bold, but also, I don't want to hear any other voices beside Connor's right now. I'm replaying our conversations and my body is doing the weird crush thing—the funny belly, lava-like heat. A lightness. I totally get why people in musicals break into song when they feel this way. So weird. This boy, I hated his guts a week ago. The this-way-and-suddenly-that-way of it all. Like Sabine, cheering one second, dead the next. Life and death rubbed up against each other, a paper-thin border between them.

I dial her number now, and she's back, telling me to give her a "G." Her breathless voice, never stopping for air. She lived in fast-motion to the end. Her cheer against my ear, I close my eyes and picture her in her final minutes. A bunch of cells dividing inside of her. A combination of her and Nick. Nick, who told her she was ruining his life. Nick, who sobbed at her service, telling my parents that he really thought they'd marry someday. Why didn't she tell me about Nick? About getting pregnant? In my head, I ask her this over and over.

She was odd that way, though. So forthcoming about losing her virginity, but taking some pill to calm her nerves. Her and Martha, always pushing the edge, and then needing something to settle them down. I remember a few days before the accident, Sabine, Martha and I rode the bus downtown to Pioneer Square. They ordered triple espressos, stirred in some brown sugar, and slammed them. On the bus home they were so amped up, they both popped little white pills. Up:Down. Crazy.

I wonder what it would be like to crave the spotlight. To want people to watch and admire you. Maybe that's why Sabine had so many secrets. She needed to keep some things locked in a place where only she had the key.

There's no way Martha knew. There can't be. She wouldn't have told Martha and not me.

There are only a handful of us on the bus when it pulls into the downtown corridor. With the twin phones, one in each hand,

I step out onto the street where a shopping-cart woman is picking through the barrel of a public trash bin. The homeless woman, who looks sixty, picks up her head and smiles at me. She says, "You gotta spare dollar for a grandma?"

I return her smile and shake my head, thinking of Nona. Nona would be crushed to think of Sabine dying not a virgin— pregnant, no less. She and her countless rosaries: the black one, the mother-of-pearl one, the one supposedly blessed by the Pope. "We pray to the Virgin, Brady," she'd said, pulling me down next to her in front of a stand of votives at Saint Mary's. "Sabine, she died a pure girl. The Virgin protects her own."

It seemed ludicrous to me that Nona and her religious ilk thought of Jesus' mother as someone who'd never had sex. Virgin:Whore. Another paper-thin border.

The 44 stops in front of me, the door gasping open. I'm a solitary rider on this bus, and it lurches along Broadway, winds around the maze of streets to Barbur, and by the time we're near my stop, I've listened to Sabine's demanding me to have a great day a dozen times. The thirteenth time I hear her, I leave a message. "Are you OK, wherever you are?" I say into the tiny speaker of my phone.

My blistered feet are swollen out of my shoes by the time I round my corner and my driveway looms into view. *Safety, danger, safety, danger,* in my head as I walk by the lawns. My house looks different somehow, as I walk toward it. Then it hits me why. Sabine's Volvo. It's gone.

Mom's sitting at the kitchen table with some documents in front of her, reading glasses perched on the end of her nose. She doesn't look up when I enter. Dad's in front of the TV in the adjoining room. He clicks it off and comes into the kitchen, where I'm rooting around for leftovers in fridge.

Nothing. Onto the cereal cabinet then.

"Where the hell have you been?" he demands, slurrily.

I don't have to get any closer to know that if I did, I'd smell beer or whiskey off of him.

"I had to meet someone," I say. "A school thing."

He slams a fist down on the kitchen counter. "I pay your god damn phone bill every month, I expect you to call when you're out late. You had me worried sick."

"Sorry," I mumble, and pour milk into a bowl of All Bran and Lucky Charms.

Dad grabs the spoon out of my hand and wags it at me. "What is going on, young lady?"

Mom slaps her pen down. "John, please. Yes, Brady, we left you several messages. It's common courtesy."

So many places I could go with this, I know. What to say. What to leave out. I squeeze a fist into my hand like I'm about to punch someone. My feet throb. "I was asked by my teacher, to go to Mrs. Cupworth's house with her. There's a to-do about the prize. I've been thinking, these last few hours, about how to handle it." And then, for good measure, and because I want to know if I, too, can play a bluffing hand, I add, "Sorry I didn't check in. My phone died."

"See, I told you, John. What do you mean, a 'to-do?'"

"Some people," I begin, "seem to think that the prize was given to Martha instead of me because if they gave it to me, it would look like hush money."

"What people?" says Mom. "That's ridiculous. I told you the whole lawsuit theory was half-baked in therapy the other day. Mr. Field showed me your grades, Brady. That's why. That's the only reason why."

Dad is trying to catch up. He's still wagging the spoon in mid-air. "You should have borrowed someone's phone. Don't they have landlines in those West Hills estates?"

"So, have you decided yet? About suing?" I want to know.

"Your father and I are at an impasse in regards to that," Mom says, her dagger-eyes peeking over her glasses at Dad.

Dad, spews, "Making her do those ridiculous stunts— that scorpion move. If for no other reason, I'd like to make people aware. Prevent another father from having to bury his daughter."

Before I can stop myself, I say, "We didn't bury Sabine. We burned her."

"Brady!" Mom cries.

In one fluid motion that only an ex minor-league baseball pitcher can pull off with grace, Dad flings my cereal spoon across the room, and backhands me right across the face.

The pain cracks through me, but I take it. I'll have a child-services-sized bruise blooming on my cheek by morning, and I'm glad. I stand there glaring at my father, who is not yet remorseful, but I know soon will be. *Rager:Regretter*, says the voice of Sabine.

"Where is Sabine's car?" I demand.

My father's hand pulsates into a fist and out of it. "I gave it to Nick," he says, before striding out of the kitchen and through the door to the garage.

I'm still in shock, my cheek stinging, when the sound of garage door ratcheting along its chain fills the room. Then Dad's revved engine, and the squeak of tires burning rubber down the length of our drive.

thirteen

There are stains the next day. On my cheek, in the driveway. Black and blue marks made by a fist and rubber tires. Mom left a note on the table.

Hope you're OK. Had to go into work early. Have asked Dr. Stern to meet us this afternoon at 4:00. Please don't be late.

My feet are two throbbing, bloody slabs of meat. There is a smear of charcoal-black under my eye and around my cheekbone. If ever there was an excuse to not go to the school … but I'm not sure I can stay home, either. Dad never returned last night, and I'm certain he'll show up, hungover and apologetic. I'm not ready to talk to him yet. With or without our therapist.

Plus, my feet the way they are, there's no way I'll be much good on foot.

In Sabine's room I find some padded Smartwool socks and the orthopedic nurse shoes she'd wear when her own feet were bunioned up from dance class. To complete the frump look, the abused housewife ensemble, I choose one of Nona's dusters leftover from her hip-surgery stay with us, under which I've donned a Spandex unitard. After I add a pair of I-walked-into-a-door sunglasses, I'm ready to go, and be the weird, artsy outcast they've come to know and avoid.

*   *   *

In school, Mrs. McConnell isn't buying it. She seems distracted all period, and her thoughts on Faulkner and duplicity and existentialism are stalled out. Even Cathi and her ever-raised hand can't get a rise out of her. I'm not surprised when, again, she keeps me after class.

"Take them off, Miss Wilson," she says, pointing at my ten dollar RiteAid shades.

My face is the sort of lopsided swollen of movie-of-the-week heroines. I can feel it. But Mrs. McConnell is an experienced sleuth. She says, "I am a mandatory reporter, you know."

"I was in a car accident," I spit out. "The other day. I was driving my sister's car, and I stopped suddenly, to avoid a dog, and my head hit the wheel. I don't have a license. My parents don't know I drove. Report if you must, I know I deserve it, but it'll only add to their troubles."

My Classics teacher ponders my lie. She's had decades of bullshit, and her meter is honed. But, I'm learning how to lie pretty well these days. Getting some sort of latent crash course. It's easier to poker-face when only half your face looks normal. Finally, after circling me, and scrutinizing my outfit, she lets it go. "Ms. Bowerman told me about the Art Show investigation."

So now it's an investigation?

"Mrs. Cupworth is rankled," I say. "But she's been very gracious to me. And Bowerman—Ms. Bowerman—too. I hope it all works out, the article. You know, with the vote coming up and funding on the line and everything."

"Well, politics aside, I'm not sure if it's the right time to be bringing you into the middle of a battle. And, I've said as much."

I'm not sure why Mrs. McConnell has taken such an interest in my well-being. Language Arts has never been my forte. I'm a solid "B" student in this class, not exactly a genius.

"Art is pretty important to me," I manage.

"I know, dear. And I've seen your work. Promising. You have an eye for truth."

An eye for truth.

"Well, if that's all, I shouldn't be late for Spanish," I say, feeling naked, suddenly.

"That is all," she says, and, before I'm truly out the door, "Brady?"

"Yes?"

She points to her eye, "When you're ready to talk about what really happened there, I hope you'll feel comfortable enough to share it with me."

After last period, I immediately dash out the main doors. Sore feet or not, I can't stand another minute in this building. I'm halfway jogging, my backpack bouncing up and down against the soft cotton of my grandmother's housedress. And then, there it is. In the school lot. Already retagged with a new parking sticker. Nick's managed to find time in the last twenty-four hours to wax it up, and it reminds me of the way dogs have to pee against every blade of grass in another dog's yard. There's even a new bumper sticker on the back. *LAX: Trample the weak. Hurtle the dead.*

Really?

My stomach lurches up into my throat. I think I'm going to vomit. I start jogging for real, and oddly, my feet feel up to the task. The *bump, bump, bump* of my textbooks up and down in my backpack only makes me run faster.

It's cool outside. Overcast and heavy. I'm not sure where I'll end up, but I keep turning corners, crossing streets. I just want to be away from people.

My backpack starts ringing.

There's a picnic table up ahead, in one of those miniature neighborhood parks that time forgot with a metal swing set and long, straight slide. By the time I extract my phone, there's a voicemail.

"Hello, Brady? This is Rory Davis, from the *Portland Journal*. I'm writing an article on the Cupworth situation, and your number was passed along by your teacher, Vanessa Bowerman. I'd love to ask you a few questions. Do you have some time to chat this afternoon or tomorrow?"

In her practiced calm reporterish voice, she left various numbers and emails, and good times to reach her. I take a breath and realize that my heart is still beating like crazy from my accidental boot camp up the hill. Everything is happening so fast. Maybe Mrs. McConnell is right—people need to back off. Stop asking things of me. I look up and watch a mother push her young daughter on a swing. The mom is very pregnant and looks exhausted. The little girl wants more action; she wants to go higher, and she's squealing "Do it harder, Mama."

I want to let that little girl know that her mother will continue to disappoint her. Not only will she make her get off the swing before she's ready, soon, there will be a needy little infant in the house gobbling up all her time. For the first time, I try to consider what it must have been like to be an older sister. To have your parents all to yourself, and then, suddenly, not have them all to yourself. Sabine must have resented the hell out of me.

I sit watching the mother-daughter show in mesmerized silence. I don't call the reporter and I don't hustle on over to the therapist's. Instead, when at last the little girl is pried off the swing a tantrumy mess, the mother yanking her down the little grassy slope, I call Connor.

He picks up on the first ring with a "Yo."

I don't bother with any chit-chat. Like Nona after the bless-me-father in the confessional, I'm right to the point. "My parents gave Sabine's car to Nick."

"Figures," he says. Then, "Want to come over?"

I'm so eager to get there, it doesn't occur to me until I'm almost at Connor's front door that I'm wearing this goofy outfit, my enormous backpack pushing me over the edge into certifiable.

The door is open a crack and when I knock, Connor's voice pierces the Beastie Boys on the stereo, "C'mon in."

Connor's house is all Stickley furniture and high-end fabrics. His mother's an interior designer, and his stepdad is an architect, so good taste is the vibe here, and it screams from every corner of the living room. Connor's back is facing me and he's fixing a sandwich on a slab of granite bar. "Hungry?" he asks.

He's wearing a thin brown tee-shirt and skinny jeans, and everything that's amazing about his body is accentuated as he puts the finishing touches on the stoner haute cuisine—a white bread PB&J, with extra J.

"I'm good," I say.

When he turns around and catches the grandma outfit, he tries to hide it, but he can't. His face explodes in laughter. He's practically snorting as he says, "Nice kicks, Nurse Brady."

"Yeah, well, my feet are all blistery from your enforced march through the woods."

"I like the apron look too," he says, stuffing a chunk of his sandwich in his mouth. "Suits you."

"What's that supposed to mean?"

"Just, you know, you've got that artsy thing going on." He reaches out to me and chucks me under the chin like you do a little kid, and, reflexively, I slap his hand down.

"Spicy," he says.

"Don't patronize me Connor Christopher."

He fake-pouts before cramming the rest of the Wonderbread. Then he says, "So, Nick's managed to finagle her car, eh? Dude's an operator."

I drop my backpack and sit down on a bar stool, facing a stainless steel appliance kitchen and a picture window that looks out over blossoming trees. "My folks seem to think he walks on water."

"You planning on sharing the counter-evidence to that?"

I shrug. Connor leans on the counter, positioning that muscular torso right at the level of my hip. His bicep is touching distance. I'm getting distracted. Connor pivots and those green eyes of his are leveled at my cheap sunglasses. "When it comes to assholes like Nick? Sometimes life catches up."

"You believe in karma?"

"Well, I'm not sure about the whole Hindu wheel thing, but I do believe in this saying I heard once, 'live by the ego, die by the ego.' That's what'll happen with Nick. He's gonna burn some bridges. Big time."

I'm wondering about Martha, and what her reaction might be to hearing Sabine's voicemails. The threats, the anger. "Did you know Martha's in the running for Rose Festival Queen?"

"Nope. I'm not really up on that community stuff, but I can't say I'm surprised."

"And, something else. Mrs. Cupworth and Bowerman want to make a big stink about the Art Fair, how that all went down. There's a reporter who wants to talk to me about it. It could get ugly."

Connor slants his head a little. Narrows his eyes. The Beastie Boys's *Mullet Head* fills the room. That meaty hand that held my sister's foot all last year while her body contorted into bends and straddles, it strokes the sore spot on my cheek

I'd all but forgotten about. And then that same hand peels off my sunglasses. His touch is soft as a kitten brushing up against a leg, but his voice goes deep and serious. "Who the fuck did this?"

I freeze. I don't even want to say it out loud. How can I? "It's complicated."

"Brady. C'mon. Don't bullshit me. I know a right hook plant when I see one."

He's calling me on it, and I don't know what to say. That my dad hit me because I deserved it? That he's a stupid drunk? The world and everything I know about it died with my sister?

It's past 4:00, and I'm sure if I looked down at my muted phone right now there'd be a few missed calls. "I think my parents are going to split up," I say, shocking myself with the words that I didn't even know were in my head.

"Welcome to the Happy-Happy Club. But that still doesn't answer my question."

I wish I could just curl up and be that little kitten I'm imagining when Connor's fingers stroke my cheek. Have those careful hands hold me, and not have to say another word. "Last night, when I finally got home, my dad was wasted and I know he'd just had it out with my mom, who, by the way, is probably cheating on him. We argued, he slapped me. Big whoop."

"Wasn't your dad some big deal baseball player or something?"

"Minors. But, yeah, he's got an arm."

"That really sucks. I'm sorry. I mean really, I apologize if I kept you out too long and that contributed to any of this…"

The trees outside are fluffy with white and pink, and that's exactly how my insides feel right now. Sore feet, sore eye and cheek, all of that is melting away. I'm sort of lightheaded, and I want to tell Connor Christopher that he's more beautiful than David. More holy than the apostles that float around on the ceiling of the Sistine Chapel. I want to sketch him. Paint him. Kiss him. Dad hitting me, the horribleness of that, it dissolves into the possibility of feeling Connor's lips pressing on mine. And then, just like that, I move my swollen, bruise-filled face toward him, and push my lips—the top one, then the bottom one—up against his.

My eyes are closed, but when I open them, I see his surprised and bulging eyes staring back. Though I haven't done a lot of kissing, I've done enough to know that in order for a kiss to really work, both parties need to participate. And Connor, he's not cooperating. His lips don't pucker, they don't push back. But they don't back away, either. Until they do. Finally. And he says, "Brady. Whoa. I was caught off guard there."

I'm sitting on a stool at the counter of the boy accused of killing my sister, wearing my grandmother's housecoat, and I've just made a pass at him. One that, it looks like, he's refusing. In all the world of awkward circumstances, there can't be any that top this. The Beastie Boys are screaming … *you don't stop.*

I wish.

"Not that I wouldn't be interested…" Connor tries.

I sigh, stab the shades back in place, straighten up. "I get it. You don't feel that way about me. No worries."

"Brady, honestly, I don't know what it is I feel for you. But it is *some*thing."

Now he's just toying with me. I can't take it. "I'm out of here," I say, swinging my legs off the stool, grabbing my backpack.

He reaches for my arm and I jerk it out of his grip. "Don't go," he says, with a question mark at the end of it.

"Look. I'm an idiot. And I'm tired of being an idiot."

But really, why I need to get out of Connor's house immediately is I'm about to sob. To scream and cry like that toddler on the swing earlier. I'm tired of being an idiot but more than that, I'm tired of being me. Connor calls my name a few times, the sound of his voice behind me like salt on my blistered feet.

fourteen

By the time I round the corner where I'd almost taken Sabine's car over the edge, my eyes are so brimmed with tears, I can't see. I'm sneezing like crazy—either the pollen or the sting in my sinuses from holding back crying. Don't know. But what I do know is that if I start weeping now, I'll never stop. The weight of everything is a cloudburst inside me. The sadness. The relentless sadness. My sister. Dad. Everything crash landing.

I miss her so much. It feels like a canyon opening inside me, as though an Exacto knife is separating organs from tissue. This must be what people feel before hurling themselves over the Vista Bridge. The two suicides at Greenmeadow this year, one was a jumper and the other, pills and alcohol. What goes through a brain on its way out? And Sabine. Did she know she was going to die in that second before her neck snapped in two? Who was she thinking about when she landed, chin first on the gym floor? What last words did she want to say amid the gasps and disbelief, the still recording camera phones? She died cheering, my sister. Encouraging her team to victory. *Never give up*, that's who she was. She died raising cheer.

Brady Brooder. The remaining Wilson girl. The half-empty sister. I feel like I'm treading water, not knowing where to go next. The rest of the world, they're getting on with it—Martha and Nick. And Mom, scheming a new life for herself. Every step I take on my sore feet seems aimless, pointless, wrong.

I continue down the hill in the direction of home. There

will be consequences for missing the session at Dr. Stern's, but I don't care. I have a paper due on *As I Lay Dying*, and I have yet to start it. I flunked another trig test. Maybe I, too, will end up at BALC, or on track for a GED. Birds are singing all around me, oblivious that the world is a festering ball of shit headed for doom. The sun breaks through the leaden cloud, like it often does in late afternoon. Why didn't Connor kiss me back?

My phone vibrates, and this time I just answer it. "This is Brady."

"Hi there, Brady. Rory Davis again. Is this a good time?"

In the end, after my twenty-minute grilling session with the reporter, my stomach is a knot of panic. Judging by the tone of her questioning, this Rory Davis wants to stir things up in a big way. *Leading the witness* is how they put it on the lawyer shows when the defending attorney screams for a mistrial.

"So, they told you you'd won, and you didn't find out they'd changed their minds until the ceremony?"

And,

"I understand that that very afternoon you were speaking with the vice principal. And he mentioned nothing, even though they'd had a meeting an hour earlier where they decided to give the award to Miss Hornbuckle?"

And,

"How did it feel, having just lost your sister in the most horrific accident imaginable, and then, having yet another rug pulled out from under you?"

The rug, pulled out from under me. My father, cracking me in the face. Connor's lips, shrinking away from me in repulsion.

I don't know if I answered any of the reporter's questions, but I do know I said more than I should have. With all the sobs, the curses, the nonsensical rant, I'm sure I sounded like a raving psycho. What would this Rory Davis make of my weepy, angry words? Did she get the story she wanted, this hungry reporter?

I conjure various headlines. *Crazy student loses prize*, or *Angry nutjob embarrasses family, self*.

But the whole thing is out of my hands now. Whatever will be, will be.

When I check my phone, there are several missed calls and messages. My parents, no doubt, are frantic. I don't want to worry them, but I also don't think I can face them today. My father and his inevitable drunken sobbing. Mom and her demanding, know-it-all action items. So I make another call.

"Nona?"

"*Nipote*. Papi and I were just talkin' about you." Her voice moves away from the phone, and I hear it shouting at my near-deaf grandfather, "Papi, Papi, Brady is on the phone, pick up the extension."

We chit-chat about nothing for a while, and then I drop the bomb. "Can I come stay with you for a few days?"

"With us? But what about school? Your Ma?"

"It's a little tense over there right now," I tell them.

"Are you in any trouble, *bambino*?" asks Nono.

"Not exactly," I tell them. "I'll take the bus over, and we can talk about it."

The buses to North Portland are not what you'd call express service, and by the time the 44 makes its way to the University of Portland neighborhood where my grandparents have lived for fifty-three years, it's well-past their supper hour.

Their neat-as-a-pin pink aluminum-sided bungalow clashes with the red sky behind it. A new wheelchair ramp criss-crosses the front of their house, and I wince thinking about them needing to use it sooner or later. Nona and Nono are plan-ahead types. They shop for Christmas in January. Get their furnace serviced in May. The front door opens a crack while I'm still making my way up the front walk, which is lined with orderly tulips.

Nona steps out on the stoop, her arms spread wide the minute or so it takes to reach her.

"My duster," she cries, as though I'd planned it, this reunion between my grandmother and her housecoat.

But, as soon as she's done hugging me, squeezing the non-bruised side of my face, she takes in a breath as though witnessing a homicide. "What happened to you?"

I think about giving her the steering wheel story, but then, I don't. "I'll tell you later. Meanwhile, have anything to eat? I'm starved."

All three of us are sitting at Nona and Nono's little boomerang table—one they've had since the 60s. My grandmother pushes bowls of macaroni and sliced ham my way. Where does all of this food come from? Nono is growing thinner and balder. He's practically nodding off at the table.

"I was so mad when that girl got your prize, you know?" says Nona all fire and spit.

"Forget it, Nona. Besides, that lady who spoke? She wants to give me an equal prize. And, she bought my drawing." I don't mention the forthcoming *Portland Journal* article.

Nona jiggles Nono's arm. "You hear this? Papi? Good news, eh?"

My grandfather nods and half-opens his eyes, tweaks my cheek. And then, "What the hell happen to your face, Brady?"

I take in a deep breath. From where I'm sitting, I can see

the shrine of Sabine. A 5x7 next to a photo-electric candle, which also features my sister's alive face. The obligatory Virgin statue, along with a stack of mass cards. *Tell them*, says the voice of my sister. *Tell them what happened.*

"I guess it was my fault," I start. "Smart-mouthing Dad. Let's just say I had it coming."

My invalid grandfather slams a fist down on the Formica so hard you'd think there was a prosthesis involved. Some robot arm jutting from his feeble body. "He hit you?"

Nona yells something in Italian. I don't know what it is, but I'm pretty sure it's some sort of curse.

"Let's not overreact," I suggest, my voice as calm as I can make it given my heart is beating all crazy in my chest. The last thing they needed was an excuse to hate my father more than they do.

"You are not going back to that house, Brady. Not until I speak with your mother," Nono says, his mouth wet with spit.

On the wall opposite the table, there hangs an oil painting of President John F. Kennedy in a skinny gold frame. One of Nona's first efforts, copied from a photograph. This is who my grandparents are. Catholics and non-forgetters. The summer of Johnsaffair, they went from being lukewarm to my father all the way down to hate. There's no going back with Nona and Nono. They know what they know.

"We're in counseling," I say, in my best Dr. Stern voice. "We're working through this stuff."

"You think a head shrinker will fix this?" Nona says, pointing to my bruise. "There's only one way to handle it. Eye for eye."

"Nona. You better not do anything you'll regret. Dad's suffering, you know?"

I'm thinking we need to change the subject. Nono seems to have nodded off again, and a small snore starts up from his place at the table. I redirect. "Let me take you to bingo, Nona. We can stop for lottery tickets."

That does the trick. Before long, I've cleared the table and rinsed the dishes. Nona has tucked my grandfather into bed, and put on a fresh face. Extra powder on her nose, her large mole now caked in beige. Arm in arm, in matching housecoats, we make our way to the Lincoln. My grandmother thinks I have a driver's license and I don't dissuade her from that idea.

Nona is chatty while I navigate the giant-hooded car through the streets of North Portland. She tells me that I'm beautiful, and that some day I'll have my pick of boys. She tells me the story that she always tells me. What a late bloomer she was, and how she didn't meet Nono until after the war, when everyone had given her up for an old maid, and once she married, at age thirty-six, she prayed and prayed to Saint Agatha of Sicily that a baby would "find a way to my womb."

Nona had miscarriages. Four miscarriages. And finally, a pregnancy that went to term. Mom. Born when Nona was forty three.

"She died a virgin," she says.

I'm concentrating on staying in my lane, and slowing down at every intersection while a line of cars grows like a tail behind me, so I'm thinking she means Sabine. Who lost her virginity in the forest, drugged out on Ruffies, by the way. But once Nona starts in with the *a life consecrated to God*, I know she's talking about poor old Saint Agatha. The patron saint of fertility and breast cancer and all sorts of women's issues. I get the breast cancer part (Agatha's boobs were chopped off because she *just said no to sex* with some dude named Quinctianus), but it seems weird to me that a saint famous for guarding her virginity would be who you pray to when you want to get knocked up.

"Maybe that's why your mother always had such a will. Like Agatha, you know?"

There's an impatient guy in an Iroc kissing the bumper of the Lincoln. I hate that.

"She was beaten and tortured and laid on the hot coals. Everything bad. But she died a virgin," Nona repeats, proudly.

I'm thinking that if Nona ever found out that Sabine was not only *without* virginity at her death, but also *with* child, it would just about do her in.

Finally, the chain-link fence of Holy Redeemer comes into view. I press down on the blinker stick, and the sports car guy behind me zooms around, leaving rubber on the road.

"You're a good, careful driver, *Nipote*," my grandmother says, patting my arm as I make my way around the potholes of the poor old parish parking lot.

While Nona's happily installed in front of a six-pack of game sheets in Holy Redeemer's parish hall, I make my way out to the stairwell to call Mom. She answers immediately.

"Thank God," she says. "I was *this close* to calling the police."

"I'm staying with Nona and Nono for a while."

"You're what?"

"Sorry I missed therapy."

"Brady. Your father and I need to talk to you. There's no excuse, of course, but he is devastated. *Dev*-astated, about the incident last night."

"You mean when he cracked me across the face?"

"He's staying elsewhere for a while. We all decided that until things cool down—"

"Cool down? Between who and who?" I can't bring

myself to say what I want to say, which is, *between you and your lover.*

"You need to come home, Brady."

"Too late, Mom. Nona and Nono saw the bruise. They know, and they won't let me come home."

I hear Mom sigh in concert with a yelping *Bingo* from the adjoining room.

And apparently, Mom hears that too. "Where are you?"

"Look, Mom, there's an article going to be in the paper tomorrow. Thought I'd give you a head's up. It's about the Cupworth Prize and they interviewed me. They might include stuff about, you know, the accident. I wanted to let you know so you wouldn't freak."

It's silent on the phone, and then, "Why would you even think about talking to a reporter given everything that's going on?"

"Everything? What do you mean, everything?"

She breathes a little heavily, like she's tugging on a boot or something and then, "OK, fine. Stay with your grandparents for now. I'll bring a bag with your clothes by. We'll talk later in the week."

We hang up, and my device immediately rings again. It's Connor. I press *decline*, turn off my phone, and join dozens of old ladies in the hall as the volunteer Knight of Columbus pulls out a little ball and calls *G 18.*

fifteen

Grieving sister wants answers is the above-the-fold headline in the Life & Lifestyles section of the paper the next morning. Smack in the middle, there's a photo of Sabine and me, taken at the Raising Cheer event a few months back. It looks like we're clinking pop bottles, all smiles and good times. Really, what was going on there? I was trying to grab a rum-loaded drink away from her. She was shit-faced, and later that night she puked her guts out. The granite countertops of Connor's house shine brightly in the background—the same setting where just yesterday, he'd rejected my kiss. And under that photo, another one. Sabine, under a tarp on the Greenmeadow gymnasium floor.

I grab the section of *Portland Journal* before my grandparents can see it and shove it in my backpack. This, they do not need. Nona is busy making eggs and bacon, wanting to send me off to school with some food in my belly. Nono is still in bed.

"I gotta go, Nona," I call over my shoulder. "I'll grab a Starbucks on the way. Can't be late for school."

"You want you can take the car, Brady," she calls. "We're not going nowhere today."

The thought of negotiating the Lincoln and its ginormous hood through the high school parking lot gives me chills. "Thanks, but that's OK. I'm used to the bus."

"I'll make sauce today," she calls out after me. "We eat at five."

*   *   *

As soon as I'm out the door, I pull the section of paper from my backpack. From the blocks of ink, I pull out my crazy ramblings: *She was my hero. So strong. So brave. Her neck snapped in half. Like a toothpick.*

And then: *She was trying to win another trophy for her squad. Nobody stopped her. She wanted to do something no cheerleader had ever done.*

And then, next to the picture of my dead sister, under the sheet of plastic, a little call-out: *She tried to hide it, but she was having boyfriend issues. Big ones.*

Rory Davis, that zealous reporter, named the boyfriend. Who couldn't be reached for comment, by the way. Probably because he was outfitting his new car with a stereo system.

What happened to the arts funding article? The entire Cupworth Prize issue was summarized at the end of the article, hidden on page eight, after all the gruesome statistics on how cheerleading is the most dangerous sport in high school. Clearly, Rory Davis saw a bigger story than the yawn-yawn of yet another school-funding piece.

By the time the bus comes, I'm pretty convinced that if I go to school today, I'll be shot on sight, so, when the 5 pulls up to the mall kiosk downtown, instead of riding toward Greenmeadow, I get off the bus. I get off with my backpack and the article about how sad and pissed off I am, and the $46 Mom put in my overnight kit plus the $29 Bingo winnings from Nona, and I'm thinking that'll buy a lot of chocolate croissants and double skinny chai lattes.

Downtown is chilly this morning. The homeless guys are still burrito-wrapped in their sleeping bags in the various doorways of semi-abandoned buildings. A few dreaded teens are setting up their panhandling stations on the busy corners by Pioneer Square. It's still too early for the Greenpeace kids, and the Sponsor an Orphan from Africa kids, but the real destitutes, the prostitutes, and the crazies are floating around amongst the gainfully employed.

I sketched here last summer. Hunkered down on the brick steps of Portland's outdoor "living room," with my graphite and my pad, I spent hours watching, drawing. There was a man with a dog—a beautiful boxer-pitbull type mutt. He called her Olive and as he sat in the sun, his shirt off and his eyes closed, he just stroked that dog like all that mattered in the whole world was the touch of that sun-kissed fur. The man was covered in ink and track marks. His beard was a scraggly mess and you could count his ribs—they were Jesus ribs, the spaces between them hollowed out and smooth. This guy, he was probably no more than 30, but missing teeth.

The dog called Olive stood and guarded this sack-of-bones guy. Anyone walked up too close to her master, she would growl a low, guttural moan. You got the feeling that no matter what this man, this obvious junkie, went through, that dog had his back. The lines and the shading and the shadow from my charcoal blended with the reality of that connection. It was like the love between those two living creatures slipped inside me and found its way out through my hand. Now the sketch is sitting on an easel in the grandest house in Portland. I wonder where the subjects are. My models. And in that wondering, I know where I need to go next.

At Blick's I buy Prang-wrap charcoal pencils. I buy a couple of sticks. A black brick eraser, a soft kneaded one. And a pad of heavy-weight paper. My left forearm always goes smudgy, so I get some free cloths from their rag bag, and some spirits to clean off all the ashy residue. The smell of oil paints and gum erasers and linseed oil—it goes into the core of me, a jolt of joy, almost a fever. It's like I feel in Ms. Bowerman's class. Home. The thereness of the world melts, and in my belly is a bed of coals, warming me for the chilly day. It's twenty-eight blocks to Forest Park, and I need to walk all of it just to settle the jumpy thoughts and ideas welling up inside me.

Slow down, whispers Sabine.

This is the most alive I've felt in weeks. Bright sun plays hide-and-seek with pewter clouds. There is such movement in the air. A gusty wind kicks up some neighborhood chimes. Birds are everywhere—a robin scoops up an enormous worm from a puddle in the sidewalk. But the worm's too big—the bird keeps dropping it, and the worm tries desperately to wiggle away only to have that robin grab it again. The bird is spring-fat, and I'm wondering if it's getting ready to lay eggs, or already has some nearby. The underbelly on that robin—the color of lips.

The sun disappears, and the bird flies away, its too-big worm safe for now, wiggling back to the trickle of water in the sidewalk crack. More breeze and chimes. I keep walking, and now I'm on a street lined with cherry trees. Blossoms pink as a prom dress are fluttering, swirling in the wind. And then, out of nowhere, the way it can be on a Portland spring day, the sky opens and pummels everything with tiny white balls.

Hail and pink blossoms pelt me—an attack of machine gun pellets. The tat-a-tat-a-tat-a-tat of them on the roofs and windshields of cars. It's deafening. My face stings with the assault. My windbreaker shields me a little, but the frozen force of the storm drills through to my bones. I keep walking toward the park.

By the time I get to the Lower Macleay sign and walk

up the trail, it's over. White drifts like seafoam fill cracks and puddles. Tender bright green fir branches are covered in a skin of ice, which is already rapidly melting. A slender rainbow arcs over the forest and bird song returns. It's a Disney movie.

Right now, I'd be in Bowerman's. But, I'm not. Brady Wilson has been marked absent yet again. I've probably missed two tests in Blue Dot trig. I'm sure I have a solid F. My stomach knots up at the thought of the *Portland Journal* article buzz at Greenmeadow. Martha must really hate me, and Nick must loathe me, and it's a good thing my phone battery is dead.

Sun finds its way to the soggy trail. My kicks make a *schlupp* sound in the muck with each step. Up and up and up and up. The little hail and wind storm has left a path of broken nature: twigs, petals, leaves. And the manmade part of it: plastic bags and beer cans.

By the time I get to the Witch's House, the sun has melted all traces of frozen white. Spring is spring again, and there's a particularly welcoming patch of grass in view of my subject: an ivy-crusted section of a dilapidated stairway. A stairway to nowhere.

I drape the plastic Blick's bag over a flat rock on that patch of grass and sit down cross-legged. Set out my supplies in a line against some chunks of basalt. Just holding my tools, smelling them. And then getting started. The way charcoal marks a blank page like a dog peeing on a bush. Indelible. Fragrant. A witness.

Sabine used to tell me that when she arched into her scorpion, she'd visualize a bird perched at the end of a twig— delicate, strong. She said that cheerleading perfection was the marriage of grace and strength. And when she got it right, the high was better than anything. As I draw my hand across the page, make the lines, and find that one place where they intersect—the one place that creates form—that's what I feel, too. Grace and strength.

The way the ivy winds and covers the stone, rising and thriving on a dead and broken thing, that's what I want. On the paper and in my heart. Blurring edges, finding perspective, recreating real.

Sun pours down now, baking off the damp, steam rising from the ground in a fog. Pencil, then stick. Eraser, then pencil. It grows. It takes shape. Stairs that end at the sky. A violent sky. Unpredictable. Angry. Then, forgiving. The ivy is holding the stones, keeping them rooted to earth. In all the world, there is not a holier feeling.

And then, soft footsteps coming up the path. The crunch and mud-sucking of someone large. And when I raise my eyes, it's a familiar shape loping up the trail. And in his hand, a white and pink, slightly soggy, Voodoo Doughnuts box. "Thought I'd find you here," he says before sliding onto the patch of grass beside me and brushing a layer of plastered pink petals from my jacket.

sixteen

Connor tells me he comes in peace, and offers a selection of Voodoo's finest, a Jimmy-studded ice cream cone, a doughnut covered in bubble gum, one sprinkled with Tang. And the signature doughnut, a voodoo doll, pierced through the heart with a pretzel rod. I point to that one. "Apropos."

"I knew you wouldn't be in school today," he says.

"What was your first clue?" I say, going back to my sketch. I don't want to make nice with Connor. Not yet.

"That's awesome, by the way," he says, pointing to the project at hand.

I shrug.

"You got some balls, girl. Calling that douchebag out. Well done."

"That comment? Not making me feel better."

He goes back to picking petals from my shoulder. Like a monkey preening its buddy for lice.

He says, "Did you collide with a Rose Festival float or something?"

"Sort of. What the fuck do you want, Connor?"

Connor drops the box of doughnuts on the grass, grabs my charcoal-wielding hand, and turns it over in his. "Delicate. But, such a mouth on you."

I want to slap him. Say, *How dare you*? I want to pull my hand away from his and keep sketching the stairway to nowhere. But, of course I don't. And why don't I? Connor's hand on my hand is sending jolts of knee-buckling electricity up and in and through.

"Here's a memo," he says, his green and amber eyes straight into mine. "I'm an idiot."

I'm not wearing a 1950's house dress anymore. The black and blue Dad bruise on me has faded. Probably what I most resemble at this moment is a molting flamingo. With black smudge on my claw. Clearly as unkissable today as I was yesterday.

"That's not news."

"Can we have a do-over?" he says, half serious and half joking.

"What, exactly, do you want to do over?"

Connor drops my hand and gently lifts my sketch pad and places it on top of the doughnut box. He stands, pulls me up and into him. Leans my head against the hollow of his neck, and just holds me, his arms around my body the way I know they held my sister. Firm.

He tangles his fingers in my hair and pulls just a little bit, so my face and his face, there's no looking away.

His breath is a little weedy, a little doughnuty. Traces of sugar on his lips. And his tongue, when it finds mine, it's the flesh of everything in nature. Wild, hungry. Spring.

I kiss back, and the parts of me know what to do, like they've gone off and taken a course in this. Without telling me. It's like my hand with the charcoal. Finding connection, language. There is no sound between us. Not one sound. Am I dreaming with the audio unplugged? It's like we're under water.

Who knows how long we're kissing? Who knows how many birds have witnessed this? How many blossoms? Hate:Love. Just like that.

Footsteps pull us away from each other. A park official looking for off-leash pets, open containers. He slows as he walks by, no doubt assessing our age and truant potential. But we're almost eighteen. We could pass for adults. For high school graduates rather than the dropouts we are.

You're not dropping out, says Sabine. Into the air I say, "Hush."

The park official marches on in his bright orange vest. Bigger fish to fry.

"Do over," Connor says. "Was worth it, don't you think?"

I'm a little dizzy. All I can muster is a nod.

Would Sabine approve? Think I'm nuts? And like he's reading my mind, he says, "I want to tell you a couple more things. They're about Sabine. And me."

I melt back down on my plastic bag, reach my hand underneath the sketch pad and into the soggy doughnut box. Before I let my teeth sink into the chocolate face of the voodoo doll, I say, "OK."

seventeen

It started at a lacrosse party. One of those crazy early summer shindigs where someone's parents are out of town and a flurry of tweets and texts commences. But, of course, Connor doesn't say *commences* when he sets the scene on how he and Sabine came to be BFFs. He doesn't say *commences*, or even, *shindigs*, but he does say *crazy*. I nod, because I remember that long-ago weekend. It was the start of the Johnsaffair summer, and Sabine was way too young to be going to those sorts of parties. And Connor was even younger. Martha was there, too. And Nick. And in case you're wondering where I was? In bed asleep, completely unaware that my sister was climbing out her window, and that she had been, night after night. Which was probably the main reason that, after she found out about Johnsaffair, Mom decided that Dad got to be the parent in charge that summer. Way out on the coast, where wild parties were sparse, and cell phone coverage even sparser.

"We were new to it, so the two of us ended up on the back deck, sort of watching all the kids get high and drunk. Back then, I didn't even know how to blaze without coughing like a girl," Connor says. And looks at me to see if I'm offended about the *like a girl* part.

He tells me all about the party. Tells me who said what, and who drank what, and who smoked what, and how Sabine looked so pretty in the moonlight, and how he felt like a bodyguard assigned to protect a movie star or a princess. Sooner or later the cops showed up, and Connor grabbed Sabine by the hand. They bolted, sneaking over a backyard fence, then, he led her to a nearby water tower where they climbed up a side ladder and hid out until things calmed down. Turns out, Nick and Martha and a few other kids got busted, and their parents had to fetch them from the Reception Center—which is Portland's euphemism for small-time juvie hall. And here is when Connor goes all starry-eyed and choked up. The glaze covering his eyes is shinier than my voodoo doll doughnut.

"I knew she would never be my girlfriend," he says. "She was sooooo … too much. Way out of my league. But when she whispered in my ear that I saved her life, and that she would never forget that, it was like some rock star up on stage picking you out of the crowd."

I'm down to the pretzel stick in the voodoo doll's heart. I can taste the frosting on my lips, and it's mixed with the taste of Connor. My stomach turns, half in jealousy and half in sorrow hearing this story. This typical story of Sabine and her effect on people. On boys. I say, "That seems like so long ago, that summer."

"She was just getting going with the whole cheerleading thing then," he says. "And she was up against girls who'd been doing it since third grade. You know how competitive she was, right? She had this whole fantasy about becoming Captain by junior year. Crazy, but she pulled it off."

I remember Connor helping her train. Running together and stuff. Suddenly, I have to know. "So you and Sabine, you never …"

He shakes his head. Connor's squatting and drawing little squiggles in the mud with a stick. "I never made a move. I knew better."

"But you would have, right?"

"Brady, stop. You know how it works. She aimed high.

Had to be with the BMOC. That's part of who she was. And what did her in, I guess."

Big Man On Campus. Nick. She started dating him the following year. His messages on her phone, so cruel and cutting. I wondered what else Connor knew. "So, what did he do to her? Besides the harassing stuff on the phone?"

Connor's face goes flat. The glaze in his eyes dries up, and he sets his jaw. "He had this jealous streak. He thought Sabine was cheating on him. He thought we were more than friends, her and me. He would threaten—like tell her that if he caught us, he'd find a way to *make it look like an accident*. That's how he phrased it. Bastard."

"Holy shit."

"Yeah."

"Did he come after you, ever?"

Connor spits. "He's a pussy. Type of guy who'll hit a girl where it won't show. That time I beat the crap out of him? A few weeks back? He's all swagger. Got nothing but a mouth and an ego."

Only a tiny bite of my voodoo doll is left. A raggedy chunk of sugar and dough. "So, like, the day of the accident, how far along was she? Who else knew?"

He shrugs. "Nick, me, a couple of Planned Parenthood receptionists. She wasn't too far gone, but really, really scared."

Sabine, knocked up and frightened; Nona and her prayers to Saint Agatha. Virginity, unwed pregnancy. Virgin:Whore. The whole complicated life of a woman made me want to go back to being a little girl. It seemed that, as a woman, there was always something to want or fear. But a second glance at Connor's lips, his eyes, and I'm back to leaving childhood behind.

"I don't think we should ever let out the stuff about Sabine's pregnancy, but I'd love to nail that so-called boyfriend of hers."

Connor nods. "He's a prick."

"He's more than that. And what about Martha? I'm sure he'll pull the same stuff on her."

"You should warn her," Connor says, stroking the tender spot on my cheek. "Have her listen to the messages."

That's what a really good friend would do, for sure. But I'm still angry with Martha. Her opportunistic nature, and the way she always comes out smelling like a rose. Part of me wants Martha to find out the hard way what Nick's all about. So. What to do? Sabine, she'd know. I listen for some advice, a whisper, and looking at Connor's quiet listening self, I'm thinking that's what he's doing, too.

And then, a question lights up in my head. "Why didn't you talk her into reporting the abuse? Did you try?"

Connor takes his hand off my face, slides it into his pocket. When he bows his head, Sabine's earring catches sunlight. Glistens. Then, he looks back up at me. "Your dad hit you, right? Has he ever hit you before?"

I shook my head. "Not even close. He's not abusive. He's, you know, grieving. Everything's out of whack at home."

"But, if you reported it, with that shiner and all? What do you think might happen?"

I touch the spot that's still sore under my eye. I can still picture Dad's face, how angry he was the other night. I run through some likely scenarios if I told the truth about this bruise. "Social services, maybe?"

Connor takes my hand now, and pets it in one direction, like a cat. "What Sabine feared more than that asshole Nick was having people think she was weak. Like, not in control of her life."

I consider this for a second while my wrist and the whole lower part of my arm goes all tingly—the hairs on it springing up. "She sure had me fooled. I mean, you'd never, ever know that *Beenick* wasn't this solid force. The perfect couple and all that. My sister, she always acted so ... together."

"Brady," Connor says. "You're nothing like Sabine that way. You, are *you*. Do you even have any secrets?"

I reach up for the dangling jewel in Connor's ear. "Besides that I'm here with you, you mean?"

He laughs a little. His green and amber eyes. That dimple. The warm glow in my belly. My heart. "So, what about it? Are you getting shipped off to your dad's?"

"Yeah, that. We're down to an ultimatum. It's back to Greenmeadow or out at eighteen."

A wave of hope flushes through me. "Would you? Go back, I mean?"

Connor shakes his head of shaggy blondish hair. "That's history."

"So, what then?"

He chuckles. "I got mad skills with a lawn mower. Know anyone who needs a yard boy?"

I look over at my half-done sketch, sitting on top of the pink doughnut box, and then back at Connor. "Looks like I'm pretty close to flunking out myself. Here I am, skipping school, and cavorting with a known trouble maker."

"*Cavorting*. Listen to you," Connor says, then gestures at my stairway to nowhere. "Seriously, Brady, you should go back. You're wicked smart, talented."

"And I just made headlines, pointing my finger of blame at the school, at Nick—who, by the way, could run for President and win. I go back, I'll be tarred and feathered."

Connor peels a couple blossoms off of me. "Tarred and flowered, you mean."

The sun is out to stay this afternoon, and in its warm glow I move in close to this boy that everyone thinks killed my sister. Some of my hail-blasted petals migrate to Connor as we hug. He feels solid and perfect against me, and I wonder why Sabine resisted him—this boy who held her in place while she cheered. Why would she instead choose the lanky body of Nick, all angles and bones?

Our lips connect again, the fullness of them together. Like a spring worm, too big for a robin's beak. And then, we pull apart. He and I, facing each other and just standing still. I see us on canvas, surrounded by a frame. It's the only way I know to make time stop. Make art out of it. Forever and ever, Amen.

And then, it's done. Just as quick as he arrived, Connor heads down the trail with his doughnut box, leaving me to contemplate the form of a stairway that stops before it reaches its right place.

eighteen

There is a car I don't recognize in Nona's driveway when I get back to North Portland. A bronze Toyota with a "Keep Portland Weird" bumpersticker. My grandparents are unaccustomed to visitors, and I get the feeling that that car has something to do with *moi*.

"Brady, your teacher is here. Mrs. Mc*Corn*ell, from your English class."

"Please, call me Beverly," says Mrs. McConnell, standing up and giving me the onceover as I walk into the living room. The smell of Italian cooking is thick. Sabine's prayer candle is plugged into the wall, her hair glows white from the little table behind the assembled Inquisition.

"Hi?" I say, biting my tongue so I won't ask why the hell she's here.

"I tracked you down, Brady," says my Classics teacher, proud of herself and obviously relieved I'm not dead or dismembered.

"Your teacher was surprised you're not in school today, *Nipote*. I'm surprised, too."

Nona has that I'm-going-to-take-a-wooden-spoon-to-your-behind look in her eye.

"It's the article," Mrs. McConnell says to Nona, whose eyebrows are all wrinkled together in confusion.

"Papi, come out, we have company," Nona hollers behind her at the hallway.

There's a noise from the bedroom. Some shuffling, and Nona excuses herself to go back to help my grandfather amble out. I talk fast. "They don't know anything about it, Mrs. McConnell, and I think we should keep it that way. They're old, you know? It'll upset them."

Mrs. McConnell sighs. "I hate to think that you're eliminating your support system, Brady. You took a risk, and I know that you'll have consequences. From your peers, at any rate. I just worry that you're cutting yourself off from those who care about you."

It makes sense, but I'm still not sure what's going on. "Is that why you're here?"

"I know it seems odd, that a teacher would follow up like this, instead of a counselor, but, you know, everyone has their hands full. It's a crazy time of year, and with the budget vote next week, so much is in the air."

I touch the lightened bruise under my eye; it's still a bit tender. "It *is* a crazy time. That's true."

"Brady," she says in a half-whisper, nervously tucking her gray bob behind her ears, "You're a bright girl. Your family has just had a devastating tragedy. One, I can relate to. I lost my brother when I was your age, and I made lots and lots of mistakes in the wake of that."

She looks fragile, my teacher, like, if given the choice, she would disappear into her sweater. This is not the *Fuck*narian scholar with the booming voice I know from class. I feel like hugging her, or at least patting her hand, but that would be insane.

"I was in the park," I say happily, hoping that I can somehow translate the positive aspect of that. "With a sketch pad and pencils. I knew Greenmeadow would be awful today, so I went and did the thing that brings me, you know, peace and joy and whatnot."

Mrs. McConnell nods, but in a sort of robot-like way, the way adults do when they're about to tell you you're an idiot. "Peace and joy and whatnot? I have nothing against that. But, Brady, you're about to flunk the semester. Don't. It'll just make things harder for you. Come back to school, and I'll get the paperwork together—an IEP or something—so you can get back on track."

An IEP. That's like being a SPED kid. Great. I get all the special ed attention, it'll be the fire instead of the frying pan. I figure as long as she's here, I might as well go ahead and ask the question I'm not sure I want to know the answer to. "Did you happen to see Martha Hornbuckle and Nick Avery today?"

Mrs. McConnell does more bob-tucking, and then my grandparents come shuffling back into the room. "Yes," is all she manages to say before Nono, both hands secured to his walker, greets my teacher in his charming, *"Buona sera."*

The table is set for four, I notice, after we bid Mrs. McConnell goodbye. And I know without asking that Mom will be joining us. To her credit, my English teacher kept mum about the article, but suggested that I discuss the current school environment with my grandparents. "I'll see you tomorrow," she said, as a parting shot, her laser eyes into mine.

Nono answered for me. "Oh, she'll be there alright. Her grandma and me, we'll drag her in by her ear."

Nice.

Nona has been simmering a sauce all day, and the basil, oregano, pork and garlic aroma is something that Jesus would die for. Really. And maybe that's why Nona's so proud of her sauce. And why Mom never refuses it. The macaroni is draining, and Mom comes bursting in, a bottle of red wine in one hand, flowers in the other, like a date.

"Sonia?" Nona says in a surprised voice. It's for show, that voice. A little game the Panapentos play. It's followed by my mother kissing the air and curtseying.

"Hi," I offer in a lukewarm voice. "You bring my charger?"

"We'll talk later," she says.

I shake a *no* into my head as Nona takes the flowers and jams them into a cut crystal vase. My grandfather returns from yet another bathroom break, the grin on his face huge when he sees Mom.

For a few years, when Sabine and I were little, we spent most of every Sunday with them while Mom held open houses or took clients around and Dad played golf. After church, Sabine and Nono would go to the market to buy vegetables and meat after dropping Nona and me here. It was Nona who first put a brush in my hand, taught me the exotic names of oil paints like cinnabar and sanguine. Vermillion and cerulean. We'd set up little canvases, side-by-side on the back porch, and if it was cold, Nona plugged in a little space heater and we'd paint in our winter coats, the old dusters she kept for paint smocks bundled around the bulk of our outer clothes. Time would melt away while we painted bowls of pears and vases of flowers. And all too soon my grandfather and sister would return and Sabine would come galloping in, asking for hot chocolate or vanilla Coke.

Something in the way Nono looks at Mom reminds me of those Sundays, and how we were all so familiar with one another. We had a system and roles and when we argued we all knew how far to take it. With Sabine gone, and Dad on the edge, and Mom all mysterious and weird, it's like someone replaced the Monthly Missalettes at Holy Redeemer with the Latin version. I don't know our new language.

The four of us sit for supper around the kitchen table,

hold hands, bow heads. Nono says, "We thank God for these gifts and for our family, Amen," and then Nona passes the salad bowl. Always iceberg lettuce, radishes, cherry tomatoes, mixed with salt, pepper, oil, vinegar. Never has there been a bottle of dressing in this house. Or a jar of Ragu.

The smell of Nona's sauce mixes with the trace of sugar that's still on my lips. The faint taste of Connor. Steam from the bowl of meat adds to the heat in my cheeks. I realize I'm giddy. This is what *giddy* feels like.

It's not until the meatballs and chunks of pork are nestled in the spaghetti that she brings it up, my mom. But, of course, she does bring it up. "Sounds like Mrs. Cupworth thinks quite highly of your talent, Brady."

"She liked that drawing of the homeless guy," I say, hoping, against the odds, that we'll close the subject.

But, no, she launches right to the heart of it. "Has there been a lot of fallout for you because of what you said about Nick?"

"Fallout?"

"C'mon daughter. Don't play coy here."

Nona says, "Sonia, what are you talking about?"

"The piece in the paper, Ma. Didn't you see it?"

Nono, through sauce-covered lips, says, "Brady, what's she talking about?"

My grandfather is the type of guy you don't bullshit. When he narrows his eyes, looks through you, all his I-came-to-this-country-with-nothing power behind it, you must speak the truth. No matter how hard. So I do. I fill in the blanks about the Cupworth Prize, that night at the Art Show, why Martha and not me—both versions, and then Cupworth summoning me to her mansion. Bowerman and her zeal to right the wrongs. That VP twerp, and then, I get to the Martha and Nick storyline. Which is the ultimate breach of loyalty as far as first-gen Sicilian immigrants are concerned. Even with Mom, sipping her wine and clucking her tongue—because, truly, she wants to believe her dead daughter's boyfriend was a saint—I don't stop until it's all out. Well, mostly out. I leave off the Connor stuff. I leave off what I know about Sabine, and the abuse, the pregnancy. But Mom, she won't let it go. She brings up the *boyfriend trouble* quote. "Why, Brady? Why would you say that?"

And this is when I make shit up.

"Sabine told me," I say. "Before she died. She said that she wanted to break up with Nick. He was jealous, and insecure, and she wanted to end it."

Liar, says Sabine.

"That makes no sense at all," Mom says. "She would have said something to me."

Nona chimes in, "Like you always shared your secrets with me, Sonia? Ha. No, a daughter at this age, she not tell the Mama nothing."

I have to agree. But I keep quiet. Drink my water and bite into a meatball. And then Mom says, "Brady, a realtor from my office said she saw you today. She was meeting a client over on Pettygrove, by the grade school? She said she was pretty sure it was you, out in a hail storm getting soaked."

Sabine's electric candle glows. Saint Agatha and the Virgin statues and that candle and Mom's realtor colleague, and even the faded oil painting of JFK, they all point their accusatory fingers at me. I'm trying to gather my words. Why don't I have words? Sabine? Help? All the way home from the park today I rehearsed a speech about school and art and why I should simply bail and get my GED and none of it makes sense, suddenly. I shift my gaze from Mom to Nona and Nono, hoping that inspiration will come, and Nono says, in a calm, scary voice, "She skipped school today. And I don't blame her. Look at her face. Look what your husband did."

"It true Sonia. Papi and I are very concerned," Nona says, crossing herself.

"Dad, you should talk. You and your belt, eh? How many times did you whip me for this and that growing up?" Mom stands up and machine guns her hand around the room, pointing to relics and photographs and various religious icons. "You hide behind all of this pious crap. So righteous. So holy. Not that it's any of your business, but John and I are working things out with a mental health specialist. John is mortified that he struck his daughter. Mortified. He's staying with a friend for now, but it's just temporary."

My heart is beating a mile a minute. A drum and bugle corps in my chest. We are having a full-fledged Panapento scene, the likes of which I haven't witnessed since the summer of Johnsaffair. Mom turns to me. "Brady, you're coming home tonight. You're going back to school tomorrow, and then we're going to counseling. Your dad has some very important things he needs to say to you."

I close my eyes and nod my head, and all I can do to quiet the craziness around me is sink into the memory of the afternoon. Connor and his lips. The way his arms felt around me. His dimple, his eyes, and my sketch of the stairway, and the sugary doughnut taste. The happiest I've been in months. Maybe this is how Saint Agatha got through her ordeal of getting beaten, having her breasts chopped off. Maybe Jesus was her Connor—her art. Some place she could go inside her head and heart that would deliver her from the present very shitty moment. *Shackle me, drag me away, but you can't have my spirit*, I think. *For this horrible reality is only temporary.*

And then, in the clock-ticking silence that follows, it's Sabine, finally.

That's exactly how I felt up there, cheering. Just before I misjudged my landing.

*   *   *

The next morning, Mom drives me to school. First stop at Greenmeadow is Call-me-Leonard's office, where his pretty young wife and his little boys in their holiday sweaters smile at us from his desk. Mom, as usual, looks fiery and gorgeous in her CAbi separates. Her eyebrows tweezed just so. And "Leonard" is openly flirting with her, his grin extra broad, and his occasional chuckle just this side of inappropriate. But Mom is most definitely not flirting back. "I want some assurances, Leonard," she says. "I will not drop my daughter into a snake pit."

"Oh, you know how teenagers are," he says, waving his hand dismissively. "This'll blow over in no time. Prom's this weekend. The kids have bigger things on their minds than the little piece in the paper."

Prom. I'd forgotten all about it. Not that anyone would have asked me. Typically, Bowerman's art class paints a mural for Prom, and this year's theme—Greenmeadow is 50—was no exception. It was supposed to be this retro *Mad Men* sort of mural. 60s prom gowns, The Beatles, maybe, playing in the background. But in light of the arts funding issues, Ms. Bowerman put her Birkenstock down. *This is one of the many things you can't have without an art program at the school.* We were boycotting Prom this year, she let it be known. And secretly, I was disappointed. I'd looked forward to sketching girls in chiffon and satin gowns. I wanted at those strands of pearls and elaborate hairdos.

"Never-the-less," says Mom. "Beverly McConnell and I have discussed an IEP. We think that, under the circumstances, allowances for Brady's recent slew of absences need to be made."

Beverly McConnell?

Mr. Field shuffles some papers. On his desk there is a bulging file with the word Wilson block-lettered on the tab. The flirting tone in Leonard's voice is magically gone. "Looks like your daughter has missed several exams. Assignments. The district has a policy on that."

"What was the name of that reporter, Brady?" Mom coyly asks.

Leonard's wife looks dreamily outward, and now her tanned photo-shopped face contrasts that of her husband in real life in his leather office chair. He's whiter than the papers in my file.

In the end, we get our IEP. I will be graded on stuff I turned in. The four weeks of missed this's and that's will be erased. It's like confession. The way Nona explains it, you go into the booth with your soul all full of black spots, spill your sins, then the priest absolves you and gives you an assignment. A bunch of prayers you have to say before you leave church. My penance is that I have to agree not to miss any more days. "From this point forward, understand?"

We are dismissed and the booth clicks shut, leaving Leonard Field to pop a couple of Excedrins.

We're in the main spine of the "E" and I'm still trying to wrap my mind around what just happened, this negotiation and all of this information, and what's next. As if in answer to that, Mom offers, "I will see you at 3:30 sharp. Dr. Stern's office."

I nod. Promise to show up, and watch my mother stride for the door, her stylish Coach handbag looped on her shoulder. And then, I promptly head off to girl's bathroom, where I'll stay until lunch.

nineteen

Somehow I make it through the school day without running into Martha. A small miracle. Mrs. McConnell is particularly animated in Classics. We're done with *As I Lay Dying*, and this month, we're delving into Flannery O'Connor. Cathi Serge's hand gets a terrific workout. She doesn't get the symbolism in *Revelation*. She wonders why there's so much violence in *A Good Man is Hard to Find*. But Beverly, Mom's apparent BFF, is undaunted. She offers quick answers to Cathi's questions, the type of answers that invite a student to read other great works for a deeper understanding. Plus, I am not kept after class; in fact Mrs. McConnell does not acknowledge me in any way.

Then, as soon as the dismissal bell rings and I head out the main door for my after-school therapy session, out of nowhere, there's Nick in my face. "We need to have a chat," he says, gesturing to my sister's car, which sparkles in the afternoon sunlight in its space in the student lot.

"I have somewhere I need to be," I tell him.

"Won't take long, Brady."

With a weird flip-flop in my belly, I follow Nick down the short, grassy slope to the car. He's got his lacrosse uniform on, so I know he has somewhere else to be, too. I cringe as I squeak open the heavy Volvo passenger door. This car, as far as I'm concerned, will always be Sabine's.

"Just what's your fucking beef with me?" Nick says the second we're both inside.

He's tall, but skinny. So skinny. Ichabod Crane skinny. I see his Adam's apple going up and down like a tumor in his throat. His ever-present sunglasses are plastered over his eyes, but I can still make out a twitch.

I say, "I know more than you think I do."

"About?"

It occurs to me, sitting in a car that my parents gave to him, that I have a little leverage. "Don't even go there, Nick. Just, it might be a good idea for you to watch your step around Martha. And, me, by the way. You want me to keep quiet about stuff, you'd better toe the line."

"What *stuff*, exactly? Who's been feeding you garbage about me?"

I pull out the phone I think is Sabine's, but it's not. It's mine, and, unfortunately, its screen is speckled with new texts from Connor.

"Connor Christopher? That fuckwad?"

"Nope. Not him. It's you, you dumb ass. Your voice on my sister's phone. Do you have any idea what my father would do to you if he heard the names you called her?"

Nick's a clenched mess right now. He's almost smoldering.

"My sister's death is partly on your hands, asshole. And if I could find a way to let the truth of that out without dishonoring her memory, I would."

Nick grabs the phone from my hand, his lightning fast lacrosse reflexes working overtime. He points to the black screen. "So, you know she was knocked up. Fine. But what you don't know, apparently, is that this worthless piece of shit was the one who got her that way."

My phone in Nick's hand seems poised to hurl my way. It looks menacing, like a stone from Shirley Jackson's *The Lottery*. My mouth must be hanging open, because Nick says, "That's right, Miss Know-it-all, this guy you're all fired up to exonerate? He's a creep. A liar and a creep."

This guy is unbelievable. I heard him call my sister names. Heard him threaten her. I hold out my hand, "Give it back, Nick."

"Oh, so now we're squirming, are we? Just what have the two of you been up to?" He engages my text history, which, stupidly, I don't have locked. And he reads.

How's your day going?

Wanna meet up?

Brady? You there?

My hands work their way to underneath the passenger seat, where Sabine kept pepper spray for those late nights she'd be out at some party in a distant and unknown neighborhood. I don't feel the spray, but my fingers find a little plastic Ziploc bag of cremains.

No way.

"Meet up? I'm sure your parents would love to know that you and Sabine's killer have some secret thing." He flings the phone back at me and it hits my A-cup chest before my hands can find their way out from under the seat.

Nick reaches across my lap and opens the door. "Gotta go. Just watch the trash talk, hear?"

I don't even have time to take in a whole breath. Suddenly, I'm standing in the parking lot watching Nick leave rubber on the Greenmeadow asphalt. My phone signals another text.

I'll be at the park later. LMK if you want to hang out.

I stuff the phone into my bag and head off for Dr. Stern.

Dad and Mom are in the waiting room when I arrive. Dad's face puffy, blotchy, he looks up like a puppy at me, cocking his head, then shaking it just a little. "Thank God," he says, and then stands to give me a hug.

I back away from his outstretched arms, and he sits back down without pursuing it.

"Thank you for showing up," says Mom, and then takes, what they call in yoga, a deep cleansing breath.

We are three separate people spread out in the therapist's green room, like disparate guests on a talk show. I pick up a torn and ragged *Good Housekeeping*, and page through it without really looking. It keeps my hands busy. Dad won't take his eyes off of me, and I know he's looking at the faint yellow bruise under my eye. Dr. Stern's door opens and a teary couple ambles out, tissues wadded in their fists. They slink quickly through the exterior door, and our therapist makes an ushering gesture. Out:In. A revolving door of pain and dysfunction.

The three of us settle on the large leather sofa across from Dr. Stern's squeaky office chair. He leans forward, his elbows on the tops of his thighs. "First," he says, his eyes over his half-glasses and searing into my face, "I want to acknowledge and applaud your presence here this afternoon, Brady."

In my head, there's the sound of cheering, like a laugh-track from an old sitcom. I smile my best good cooperator smile. But really, wedged between my parents, all that's going through my head is Nick. His, *I'm sure your parents would love to know that you and Sabine's killer have some secret thing.*

"John, now would be a good time for you to say what you need to say to your daughter."

Dad starts to reach his hand toward my lap and then stops it in mid-air. I swallow hard and look his way a little, but can't really bring myself to witness the pain in his eyes. He says, "Brady, I am so very, very sorry that I hit you the other day. There is no excuse for it. None. I'm ashamed of myself."

I hear Mom uncross and recross her legs. Dr. Stern's chair squeaks.

"I'm sorry I said that thing about Sabine. And I'm sorry

that I didn't call and let you know where I was that night."

Mom: It really is a worry to us when you disappear.

Dad: We love you so much.

Mom: But you need to be a little more sensitive to the situation. Less self-absorbed.

Dad: Sonia. Please. Let's keep this about my apology.

Dr. Stern: That's a good idea.

Mom: Sorry. Sorry. Yes, you're both right. So. Brady, clean slate?

Clean slate? OK, I think. You asked for it. Why not? Connor and his *Do you even have any secrets?* butts up against *But what you don't know, apparently, is that this worthless piece of shit was the one who got her that way.* All I know is that this confession booth is closing in on me. I am tired of secrets. So tired of them.

"I've been spending time with Connor Christopher," I say, just like that.

Not even the squeak of the therapist's chair. No yipping spaniels from the doggy daycare next door. It's like it is in church, when the priest raises a goblet of wine up to God and waits for the altar boy to ring the bell.

Finally, "Who?" from Dr. Stern.

"You're *seeing* Sabine's …?" says Dad.

"Not *seeing*. Just hanging out with."

"Brady, why? Why would you do that?"

"To find out more."

"To find out more, what?" Dad sputters. "More about smoking pot and not giving a shit about anyone but yourself?"

"Dad…"

"Really, Brady, how could you?"

Dr. Stern intervenes with a fingers-in-his-mouth whistle. "Let's back this truck up right now," he orders. "Brady, catch me up. Connor is, was, your sister's stunt partner?"

I nod my head, which feels, suddenly, too heavy for my

neck. I close my eyes. "Everyone thinks it was Connor's fault. The accident. But it wasn't."

"The accident." Dr. Stern says. "Sabine's fall." He's paging through old notes in his leather notebook, fast and furious. "The allegation, or, the assumption, I guess, was that the young man was high, and bungled a crucial move?"

Dad bursts in, "That's what happened. He was supposed to catch her. I was there. Her mother was there. We saw it. Brady, you saw it too."

The bone-crushing truth. I was there. But, I didn't see it. I wasn't watching.

"And this young man," Dr. Stern says. "He tested positive for marijuana?"

I chime in, a cheerleader myself for the losing team. "You guys know, right? That weed stays in the body long after its effects wear off. He swore to me he never got high before a meet or a game."

"I don't believe this," Dad mutters, anger gripping his voice. "That little shit. Not enough he takes our Sabine, but now he wants to bullshit the blame onto ... who, exactly?"

Then, like it just occurs to Mom, the solving of a mystery, she *ahas* her way into the conversation. "That's where you were yesterday? On your way to meet Connor? Instead of at school? Brady, tell me you're not romantically involved with this boy."

"What?" bellows Dad.

It's all much too much. It's crazy and fucked up and out of control, right here in the sanctuary of Beaverton Grief & Family. I gather my stuff—my book bag, my jacket, and rip myself off the therapist's couch like a patch of Velcro. *Brady, wait*, I hear behind me as I scoot out the door. "Let her go," says Dr. Stern, and those are the last words I hear before popping out to the humid and heavy May air. When I pull out my phone, more texts from Connor. I text him back, *Witch's House. OMW.*

twenty

In the end, Natalie couldn't take the stepkid thing. But that's not how it was spun. The version of Johnsaffair that hovers on the mantel above the Asian crockery mother ship of Sabine's ashes is the lie that Mom and Dad settled on. One that was acceptable because it allowed Dad to move back in and life to go on as if Natalie never happened. And the kernel of the lie was, John and Sonia loved their girls too much to split up.

For us, for Sabine and me, it was a free pass. They'd put us through hell that summer, and so, all that fall, *Sure, why not?* was the party line when we asked to stay out past curfew. Mom and Dad had various date nights and took photography and cooking classes together—trying to reinvigorate their relationship. He taught her how to golf, and she hauled him along to her open houses. They stopped short of a ceremony to renew their vows, thank God, but all we had to do if one of them refused to let us go to a party or a school event was to pout and shed a tear about the crappy summer just past, and, like magic, the verdict of *no* was reversed.

Walking up to the park to meet Connor, I wonder more about whether Mom is trying to even the score. *Eye for eye*, like Nona says. Is Mom seeing someone to get even with Dad? And, years ago, did she marry Dad, a non-Catholic, to punish her parents? Did Bowerman contact the *Portland Journal* reporter to get back at Greenmeadow's administration? Is Martha trying to prove something to Sabine, even now that she's gone? And Nick. Did he tell me that lie about Connor to ensure my silence, or because he really believes it? It can't be true, after all. I want to believe it isn't true. I need to believe that Nick is the liar. That Connor wasn't lying when he told me he never had sex with my sister.

The sidewalks are still covered in fallen blossoms, but now, instead of fresh pink, they're greyish or brown. It's all so fleeting, how beauty screams loud, then withers and dies. How one day everything seems possible, and little cubes of happiness tinkle around inside you like ice in a glass of fresh-squeezed lemonade, and then, just like that, the ice melts and the beverage grows a skin of mold. My backpack is grinding into my shoulder blades. My feet are the next round of blisters. I've done so much walking these past weeks.

The park is full of dog-walkers and joggers. An entire track team from Lincoln High School runs down the trail in a line. Rhododendrons bloom their ridiculous hues of magenta, fuchsia, and clot the edges of the park. A bee hovers over a patch of tiny daisies. Warm spring evenings, Forest Park is as busy as a mall at Christmastime. Boy Scouts earning badges tear ivy from fir trunks. Moms trying to burn off belly fat push all-terrain strollers up the path, their ponytails bobbing and wagging behind them. Everyone in Portland is here today, it seems.

I trudge the half-mile up to the Witch's House, and instead of Connor, there's a little kid's birthday party. A blanket spread out, and helium balloons tied to the lower branches of a nearby tree. Small children with missing front teeth, cone-shaped party hats on their heads held tight by elastic bands on their chins, are playing hide-and-seek all around the demolished structure. Their anxious moms yelp,

"Be careful around those metal spikes."

"Tommy, tie your shoe."

I reach in my pocket for my phone, and text, *It's a zoo up here. Where are you?*

But he doesn't text back, because he's coming up the path now, and I hear his voice, that perfect blend of tenor and baritone, low, soft. "'Bout time."

When I turn around, any lingering worry about Connor melts. The tee-shirt that hugs his chest, the muscles on his arm. That dimple the size of a grain of rice. Those lips. But we don't kiss, not yet. We are still shy with each other. That after-the-first kiss shy that's like early blossoms, not quite unfolded all the way. But what he does do is so sweet. He pulls my heavy backpack off of me. Loops it over his own shoulder, one of them, because it's too small to stretch over both.

"Where to?" he asks.

I don't want to be in this crowd. I want Connor all to myself, plus, there's so much I have to say to him. Nick, my parents. Where to begin?

Into my non-answer he says, "Got my stepdad's truck. Let's jet."

Back down the trail we go, toward the small semi-circle parking lot. It occurs to me that I must look like hell. My emerald hair has faded to puke green, and I can see the pickety strands of it pointed down over my shoulder to my no-boobs-to-speak-of chest. The hole in my Keds is frayed the size of a big toe. I'm wearing an old dress of Sabine's, paired with polka dot leggings.

And then, halfway back down, he reaches for my hand. His fingers weave with my fingers. The awkwardness of two different sized people on uneven ground holding hands. My palm sweats. And before we even get to the truck, I ruin everything by blurting, "I need you to tell me the truth."

"About?"

"Sabine. You. The two of you."

He keeps holding my hand, but his eyebrows squinch. "I did. Tell you the truth."

I realize that every step I take with him down this trail makes it harder to face the possibility that I'm being played for a fool. What if I'm wrong? What if Connor is a liar and Nick is telling the truth?

Listen to your gut, says Sabine.

Two men barrel past us, looking at the insides of their wrists at fancy sport watches while they huff and puff. I pull my hand out of Connor's and fold my arms as though suddenly chilled by the breeze made by bodies running past. Connor has to be who I think he is. He just has to.

It takes a couple of tries to start the engine, and then we're sputtering along the 30, headed to Heron Island, a few miles northwest of town. He's made a deal with his parents, Connor tells me. He's got a couple yard jobs, and he gets to pee in a cup every once in a while, and as long as he's clean, as long as he makes enough money for gas and insurance, he can live at home. He seems pretty happy about it, this new plan. And, I can't help but be happy too. Until I replay the conversation with Nick, and the scene at Dr. Stern's.

We cross the bridge to the island, and head to Heron Lake where Connor tells me the coolest birds live. "The way you are about colors, you'll be amazed," he says. "They're like this brownish-red with fluorescent green stripes."

I nod and lean back, happy to not be walking. The truck is noisy and bouncy, there's a lawnmower and weedwhacker in back clunking against the metal sides of the pickup. But the sound is somehow soothing in its realness, and just for a minute I imagine what it would be like to live out here on one of the farms we're passing. Spending the day watching birds and driving a tractor through all the furrows and dips of the land.

The early evening sun is a ball slowly sinking, and it doesn't even matter to me where we are heading and when we'll get there. There are more pink blossoms out here. Darker pink than in town, fringing the branches of wilder, bigger trees. Connor's hand is busy with the shifter, but in between gear-changing, he rests it lightly on my leg. It feels old fashioned, sort of. Like one of those Saturday Evening Post photographs all sepia and sentiment. Or maybe a Hallmark card. A low, slow jet flies overhead. A "V" of geese shares the sky with the plane. Their honking pierces the noise and clunk of the truck. It occurs to me that we've been driving for a while. "Why all the way out to Heron Lake?"

He says, "We can see all three mountains from out here. And the water birds."

Sabine and I spent some time here last summer. A couple of parties. Then, I remember. "You waterskied here. Last August, right? At the cheer retreat weekend?"

He smiles, and points to his ear, where Sabine's earring wags just below his lobe. "That's when she gave me this. Made me wear it, a girl's earring. I lost the bet we had that she wouldn't get up on one ski by the end of the day. She did, so I had to agree to wear this forever more."

Ah. A bet made with a lie. "Connor, you're a rube. Sabine's been skiing on one ski since she was eight."

He seems genuinely surprised to hear this. A little sad, too, his eyebrows squinch up again.

We pull off the main road and onto another, smaller road, and drive under a canopy of enormous oaks, half-naked with leaves just beginning to dot the lacy branches. The road turns to gravel, and gets one-lane narrow. Connor shifts to second and I feel my body jiggling around inside my clothes. After weaving around potholes and nearly squashing a big yellow racer slithering across the road, we come to a small, gravel lot. Connor cuts the engine and the truck knocks and rattles a couple of times. Behind the bench seat is a little basket, and Connor lifts the lid of it and takes out a plastic Subway bag and a couple bottles of flavored ice tea.

"A picnic?"

"You do eat, right? I saw you inhale that voodoo doll yesterday. Don't know where you put it, but, hey. Hope you like ham."

We climb out of the truck and I follow Connor along a path, and then we bushwhack a bit over dead blackberry vines. Newly born blackberry vines are sprouting fiercely from the dead ones. Large flowers—again, pink ones—pop out the ends of the prickly vines, which are tender, but even so, they catch Sabine's dress and my leggings and snag as I rip through. At the end of a short trail, we're there, at the edge of Heron Lake. It's late enough, so all the hikers and birdwatchers are gone. Just a couple of older guys in hip-waders sinking their fishing lines into the overgrown pond. But what's most amazing, when we find a flat rock to settle on, are the mountains. In the faint glow of daylight, there's the cone of Mt. Hood, backlit and majestic and still covered in winter snow. And to the left of that, the flat-top of the volcano that rocked the world a few years before I was born. Mt. Saint Helens. And furthest away, in between St. Helens and Hood, is a big hump that you might mistake for a fluffy cloud unless you knew it was Mt. Adams. The reason the cheer team came here for their retreat is obvious. The Cascades and their bigness, the way they make you feel resurrected and lucky to live here. Those mountains are what the squad aspired to. Heights. Domination. Awe.

My stomach is a knot of sorrow, and it happens so suddenly. Just as quickly as the miracle of this setting seeps into my bones, I'm left empty. Drained. And it's because of this I need to scoot closer to Connor. I need to feel the solid weight of him against me. Reassurance that the earth hasn't deserted me. He opens an arm and locks me up tight against him. Separate:Together. Herons teeter in the rushes. The teals with their cinnamon and green heads sit on the quiet surface of the water, occasionally dipping their beaks in for a drink. More geese, overhead. We sit there for a few minutes, sharing food.

And then, because I have to, I tell Connor about earlier in the afternoon. About Nick and what he said. I tell him about the horrible therapy session where we had to relive the accident. Talk about *that day*. I know I'm crying without thinking about not crying, which is a weird feeling. It just comes, the tears. The sobbing, choking blubber sounds from my throat. "I can't stop missing her. I keep waking up every morning, and have to re-realize she's gone."

"Brady," Connor says, holding me, squeezing me, really, against his ribcage. "Do your parents have any idea about… this? About us?"

I'm trying not to sob, but it's not working. In between blubbery bursts I try to explain how my parents are still locked up in the idea that they have to blame someone for Sabine's death, and it'll take a while. Especially if we're keeping her pregnancy and all the Nick stuff secret.

"You do believe me, right? Brady?"

I nod, even though I'm still not completely sure.

He puts both his hands around my shoulders and pivots so we're eye to eye. "I don't want you to think less of your sister. Hear me? I mean, she is, she was, amazing. In so many ways. But underneath all that toughness, that having-the-world-by-the-balls way about her? She was fragile."

"Fragile? Sabine? Not a chance."

"Brady. There's more to it. Sabine, and how she got caught

up in a sort of game with Nick."

"What do you mean, *game*?"

And then, Sabine's cheer partner tells me more.

It's dark by the time we get back to the truck. There's a full moon, and it's a close one—bright white. It rises like the reverse of the New Year's Eve Times Square ball as we drive back across the island bridge. The bank of trees on the other side of the highway is outlined by the moon, and I'm wondering how I could sketch this. It would be a study in negative space. Shades of black and gray and just tiny bits of white.

We are quiet with each other, Connor and me. The clank of the yard tools in the truck bed is an oddly soothing sound. For the first time, my sadness for Sabine has moved away from me missing her, to me feeling sorry for her. More than *sorry for her*, really. I reach for an SAT word that means pity. *Abject* pity. With anger thrown in. Pathos? Sabine will always be my frozen-in-time teenaged sister. The milestones I'll get to that she never will. Legal drinking age, college. If what Connor says is true, she was pretty mixed up about things. Untrusting, competitive, vengeful. I don't want to believe those things about Sabine. I want to believe Nona's rendition of her. The electric candle version. The Saint Agatha pureness of her. Not this *Fuck*nerian image of a girl who would pit people against one another. A girl who would try and make her boyfriend jealous by using her so-called best friend as a … a what? A patsy? A tool? She told Nick that Connor could be the father of her baby. *Could be*, she'd said. And Connor, poor Connor, was caught in the middle.

Whatever betrayal Connor may or may not feel, none of that came out when he told me that Sabine used him to get at Nick. That she wanted to test Nick's love for her by lying about their relationship. Love? How could Sabine think that what she and Nick had was love? And how could Connor let her do that to him?

Cheerleading, Sabine told me once, is about raising belief. Making anything possible. Down by three touchdowns? No problem. Give me a "G." The smile never leaves. No matter what. "People want to be transported," Sabine said. "They want hope kept alive. That's my job."

Her job, apparently, was also to keep doubt alive. In the mind of one Nick Avery.

Finally, when we're close but not spitting distance close to my house, I move my hand on top of the one that's working the shifter. "Thank you. For all of it."

Connor doesn't really answer, but he smiles just the tiniest bit.

"You can let me out here. And, I think I may have a client for you. For the gardening, I mean."

Connor pulls to the curb and eases the truck to neutral. He turns to me. "Man, I really want to get high right now."

"Yeah. Well, that's something you've got to figure out, I guess. But, you know, Sabine was luckier than she knew. To have you in her world, I mean."

He leans in and I lean in, and like they've been doing this for years, practicing, our lips make perfect contact.

twenty-one

The next couple of days are a blur. Mom and I have a cold war at home. Don't ask, don't tell. She's doing her realtor thing, mostly, and I come and go. I attend all my classes. I do homework, even. Study. Pass tests. Martha, if she hates my guts, she doesn't let on. She's her usual positive self. Even more so, because she's got the Rose Festival thing going on. That, and she and Nick are going to Prom together Saturday, and because they're the new "it" couple, *Marnick*, good behavior is a must. When I see her in trig, she practices her Rose Festival Queen smile. And, I see her sneaking her Xanax or Ativan or whatever it is under the lip of the desk. Popping pills to keep from chewing her fingernails to stubs.

The other thing I do is I get Mrs. Cupworth to agree to consider hiring Connor for her yard. Even though Mrs. Cupworth has a crew the size of the Whitehouse Secret Service to tend her lawn and trees and flowers, I convince her that she could revitalize the herb garden alongside her portico. And the dead arborvitae in Grecian urns that surround a side patio could be swapped out for new ones. And then there're her roses.

"Is he trustworthy?" she asks when I call her.

"More than anyone I know," I assure her.

"Saturday afternoon at two," she says, and, before hanging up she adds, "*if*, you'll also agree to consider the studio space I suggested. On a trial basis, of course."

Bowerman had tipped me off about this idea Mrs. Cupworth had been "bandying about in her head." She wanted to launch an artist-in-residence program whereby aspiring artists from Greenmeadow could apply to have use of her studio—a converted pool house, actually—for each school semester, as well as through the summer. She would supply the tools of whatever medium the artist required—paint, canvas, clay—and in return the artist would spend time making art. The artist would also agree to do some public speaking in support of arts education around the city. I was the hoped guinea pig. I had to admit, the most compelling part of the offer was that she wanted me, not Martha.

Saturday afternoon, I pack up my sketch pad and my charcoal. I'm going to "feel the space out." But, mostly, what I'm hoping to do is get Connor a job that's conveniently located to where I'll be spending afternoons and weekends.

When I get to Cupworth's, I see the front of the beater truck already parked in the semi-circle, half-hidden behind a fountain that's a leaping salmon made of copper. The water spraying out of its mouth is greenish. I say a little Nona-type prayer that the truck isn't leaking oil all over Mrs. Cupworth's driveway.

I expect to see Connor still behind the wheel, waiting for me before meeting his prospective employer, but he's not in the truck. As soon as I round the edge of the circle, I hear Mrs. Cupworth's fancy old lady voice, and then Connor's mellow boy voice. They are discussing grass length. And whether it's too early to put in tomatoes.

Connor's arms are folded, and he's attentive as Mrs. Cupworth points to various places around her garden. They both look up when they hear my footsteps on the gravel.

"Good afternoon," says Mrs. Cupworth. "Your friend and I were just getting acquainted."

Connor winks at me and my stomach goes all liquid-mush. He's wearing a turned-around Mariner's cap and a bright blue shirt with the sleeves rolled halfway up his forearm. He looks like a guy ready to build something, with a Leatherman fastened to his belt and his heavy work boots. And next to him Mrs. Cupworth looks even more delicate than usual in her pale purple pleated skirt and cardigan. A strand of pearls hanging primly at her collar bone. Matching earrings. Connor is not, thank God, wearing Sabine's earring. Even for an arts lover, that might be asking too much of Mrs. Cupworth.

"When can you start?" she asks Connor.

"Now?" he says.

"Good," she says, and then extends her fine-boned, liver-spotted hand. *Don't crush it*, I think, as I watch Connor shake it in his meaty paw.

With Connor's weed whacker whirring in the background, Mrs. Cupworth leads me to the pool enclosure. The lap pool is still covered for the season, and might be covered all summer, she lets me know, since her grandchildren are away at boarding school in France or somewhere. At the far end of the pool—which is flanked by gargoyles and ornate hedges—stands a rock and clapboard cottage, the kind you see in photographs that feature the Kennedys enjoying their summer holidays. The little house has a forest green door and matching shutters, and like the main house, there's ivy growing up on the side of it. I must have gasped, because Mrs. Cupworth asks me if I'm all right. If I need some water.

I'm speechless, and for a second, can't remember whether to shake or nod my head to let her know I'm fine.

"I know it's a bit crude," she says, unlocking the heavy wood door with a little gold key, "and the lighting could be better, but the *feel* of the place. Well, it always spoke to me."

Inside, it's two big rooms, one of which has a large south-facing window and a view of Mt. Hood. Plank floorboards, the kind that are made from old growth trees, gleam like butterscotch. An easel is set up facing the window, and there's an enormous waist-high table in the middle of the space. It's like an art supply showroom in here, with stacks of paper, a crock filled with sable brushes, tubes of oil paint.

"Wow," is all I can manage to say.

"It does get a little chilly in here," Mrs. Cupworth chirps. "I have a floorboard heating system, but you'll need to dress warmly when it's overcast or rainy."

There's no way Mrs. Cupworth would know about Nona and I bundling up all those Sunday afternoons to paint on her back porch, but I say, "I'll feel right at home then."

"So, you like it? You'll try this out?"

I feel like hugging this blue-haired angel. This benefactor. "You'd really let me work here? Sketch and paint and draw?"

"Child," she says. "It would give me great pleasure to see more of your work. I think about how, in our culture's heyday, these sorts of sponsorships were ubiquitous. It was an imperative. And now, what do my peers fund? They put money in the pockets of politicians who promise to give them a break on their taxes."

Mrs. Cupworth pulls a long sable brush from the bouquet of them in the red crockery. "I tried, you know. I tried art school. Painting. Just because one appreciates, there's no guarantee of talent or success. I spent decades in bitter seclusion before I realized that there was another way to bring the beauty I sought to the world."

There's a knock at the door. It's Connor, with a question

about fertilizer. Organic or regular, he wants to know.

"Shit's shit," says Mrs. Cupworth, and both Connor and I burst out in laughter.

"Why don't you settle into the feel of the place, Brady," she says. "And you, Connor, help her move things around to her specifications."

And with that, Mrs. Cupworth glides out the door, leaving Connor and me alone, in the most magical art studio ever.

Connor helps me rearrange the table and the easel and a few large canvases. We are truly on our best behavior, and it's just the sheer awesomeness of this place that keeps me from wrapping my arms around him and burying his face in kisses.

"So, she's just letting you use this place to do art? Like, for nothing?" Connor says.

I can't believe it myself. "She wants to do this regularly. I'm her beta artist, I guess."

Connor runs his hand over the wood sash of the big picture window. "Clear vertical grain," he says. "This is probably from an ancient fir. Look at those lines."

He turns around and puts his hands on my shoulders. "So, are we good?"

I answer him by leaning in and touching his cheek with my lips, slow, soft. I wish I were the sort of girl who wears lipstick, so I could leave a mark. "I think you won her over," I tell him. "You charmer, you."

"I do know my rose cultivars," he says, thumbing invisible suspenders. "My mom's been in the garden society since I could walk. She used to take me to Washington Park, and teach me the names of all her favorite bushes. The floribundas and the climbers. Turns out Mrs. Cupworth is a tea rose fan. I told her I could get her double delights free of rust and blight."

The sun catches his cheek and there's a bit of peach fuzz and a tiny growth of whisker on his jawline. The play of shadow in this space is fantastic, and so I blurt, "I want you to model for me."

His eyebrows squinch. "Seriously?"

"Yeah, I mean, why not? You can be my muse."

He laughs a nervous laugh, "I thought muses had to be chicks. You know, goddesses and whatnot."

"Get with the new millennium, Christopher. This chick is calling the shots."

A red blush spreads across his face. "Not, you know, naked, right?"

I think about this, truly. The beauty of this boy's body, in the Classic sense. And then I think about something Bowerman once said about the difference between art and porn. "It all has to do with the intention," she said. "Is it to stir the soul, or gratify a transient urge?"

Connor, naked, well that might blur the lines. "Not naked," I say. And then, watching him push the cap back on his head, his arm flexed, I get an idea. And for the next two hours, Connor is standing at the window, Mt. Hood and its craggy cone, its white and its shadows, majestic in the space behind him. His arms up over his head and his expression like an eagle, set on something in the distance.

twenty-two

By the time Connor's arm is about ready to fall off, and my hands are black from charcoal, and Mrs. Cupworth has come and gone several times, bearing limeade and teacakes, apparently thrilled that I've taken to the space—that my "artistic sensibilities have been stirred," it occurs to me that if we were normal Greenmeadow juniors instead of outliers and freaks, we'd be getting ready for Prom.

"I'm sort of curious about it," I admit to Connor, clinking ice in yet another tall glass of refreshment. "Are you?"

Connor is rubbing his arm. "Nah. Not really."

"Oh, come on. Don't you wonder what Cathi Serge and Walter Pine are wearing? Maybe his and hers Amish outfits?"

Conner feigns shock at my cattiness. "That's not very Martha of you."

"Speaking of Martha. I'm not feeling really great about keeping quiet on what I know about her boyfriend. If anyone needs to hear what's on Sabine's voicemail, it's her."

Connor considers this, running his hand through his hat-hair. "She made her bed," he says. "As they say."

"Still. Maybe we should, you know, take a drive out there. Watch the action from afar?"

"Where's it at again?"

That's the thing about Connor. Some things he's just clueless about. The whole school had been buzzing about the unprecedented venue, the Multnomah Country and Golf

Club, in lieu of the usual converted gymnasium. This year, it was a combined deal. Juniors and seniors together, plus their dates. Tickets were $75 a piece. They were serving prime rib. And for the vegans, there would be some sort of casserole. "Made from Parisian mushrooms," I tell Connor.

"Yeah?" he says. "Well, if you want to. I think the whole thing is sort of lame."

We bid Mrs. Cupworth adieu. Connor will return tomorrow, he tells her, with his gas-powered hedge trimmers. He'll take care of that unwieldy laurel. And me, I couldn't be happier with the set-up. "You'll have to drag me out of here," I offer, and even though I'm smeared in black like a chimney sweep, she takes my one hand in both of hers the way fancy old people do, and she tells me how happy she is to hear it.

We're back in Connor's noisy truck, and rumbling down Mrs. Cupworth's driveway before I realize that, in these past few hours, I've not thought once about Mom and Dad or school. And only a little bit about Sabine. It's been an afternoon of happy normal.

Also, I'm feeling almost like Connor's my boyfriend, him driving all sure of himself in this big old truck and me riding shotgun, trying to tune in something reasonable on the crappy radio. We could be like that old John Mellencamp song about Jack and Diane. He must be feeling it too, because in between shifts he squeezes my knee and sort of glances over at me.

It's just about dark again, and if we hurry, we'll probably be able to catch some of the prom-goers climbing out of limos, their corsages pinned neatly to their vintage bodices in keeping with the 60's theme. I'm pretty sure Martha will be wearing some original gown proffered from eBay. A frock that might have cost the sum total of the Cupworth Prize. Or more.

And for Nick, maybe she scrounged up a Nehru jacket, one of those coats with a Mandarin collar, circa British invasion.

Certainly they wouldn't take Sabine's Volvo. Or even Martha's zoomy little Beemer. No, they would most likely rent a classic vehicle, some mid-century boat of a Chrysler with sharp fins and shiny chrome. Dusk has turned to coal black, and Connor asks me again if I'm sure I want to head to the country club. If I'm certain I want to stir the Greenmeadow pot. I am. Pretty sure. Even if he's not.

"What you told me last night, about Sabine and her need to play with fire?"

"Yeah?"

"Maybe that stirred something in me. Like, she was so much more of a risk taker than me, you know? Always pushing the envelope. The whole, *she lived on the edge* thing."

"Brady," Connor reminds me as we round the corner to the swanky country club, "people don't always do edgy things because they're brave. Sabine was scared to fail. It drove her to do stupid shit sometimes."

It's true, what Connor says. And I'm remembering how, in middle school, she'd play the Eraser Game with the boys. How it went was, you'd have someone rub a pencil eraser hard on your arm while you drilled through the alphabet, A through Z, coming up with words that started with all 26 letters in turn. The person with the biggest wound at the end of the game, won. And if you made the person who was erasing your arm stop before Z, you were a total pussy. It was the stupidest game ever, but Sabine always had something to prove. She stopped playing it after joining the cheer squad. There were other ways to be best, ones that didn't involve being disfigured.

We stop at the edge of the driveway into the club, and pull off the road onto a maintenance path. With the yard tools and mower in the back of Connor's truck, no one will really suspect we aren't simply the contracted help, working after hours to deadhead the rhodie blossoms and keep Multnomah Country and Golf Club well-tended so the wealthy can enjoy perfection while they whack those little white balls.

We scramble out, and dart through the bushes and between trees like stealth troops in combat. The charcoal on my hands feels like part of the costume. Cat burglars on the prowl. Connor has traded his Mariner's hat for a black ski cap. All we need are walkie-talkies, but, of course, we have iPhones.

The clubhouse is lit up with Christmas lights and candles, and as we approach it, I begin to feel a surprising sadness wash over me. Brady Brooder, always the outsider. Why wasn't I wearing a sequined, feathered, cocktail dress? Where was my tulle skirt and sweetheart neckline? My strands of pearls and velvet hair tie?

Prom, for me, was all about the outfit. For years I drew elaborate gowns in my notebooks. Princesses and starlets, goddesses and beauty queens. As we inch closer to the action, Connor and me, I get sadder. Sabine was so looking forward to Prom. She'd had a dress on back-order, and had already made an appointment with the hairdresser. Things you realize when someone dies—there are appointments to cancel. Mail from prospective colleges just keeps coming, addressed to Sabine Wilson. Cheer camp brochures. Invitations to apply for a student credit card.

Mom made a dozen copies of the death certificate, sending them hither and yon. Like birth announcements in reverse. Where it would say weight and length on a birth certificate, there is a fill-in-blank line for cause of death. In Sabine's case, complete internal decapitation.

Connor slides in next to me as I crouch behind a golf cart. Limos pull up, and all our peers spill out of them, one after the other. Up-dos, tuxedos, long and short gowns. Some girls are like storks, pegging along on heels too high for them. Others are wearing modest pumps. The boys are all over the map. Everything from super formal to polo shirt and Dockers. I glance over at Connor, wondering for a second which way he'd go. Sport jacket, probably. I don't see him in a tux.

He crawls the fingers of his hand over to where they find mine. He whispers, "Seen enough?"

I shake my head, and then, my phone vibrates. I look down. Mom. Figures. I told her I'd be home by nine, and it's ten after. I push the *I'm not answering this* button, and continue gawking at the prom attendees. So far, no Martha and Nick.

"Would you have gone?" I ask him, as Walter Pine slinks out of his mother's sedan, yanking Cathi Serge by the wrist. They look good, actually—fashionable, even—which annoys me. Walter's hair is slicked, and he's wearing a plaid cummerbund. Cathi's hair is ringlets, and aside from the poufy sleeves of her gown, she looks pretty awesome.

"Maybe. I already had a date lined up."

"Who?" I demand, louder and more jealous than I should.

"Melinda Root."

Oh. Another cheerleader. "Isn't she going out with Tom Aceno?"

He nods. "Now she is, yeah."

Connor's stock was pretty high before the accident. And me, I was popular by association. The little sister of the Class Hottie. The designated licenseless driver, just a phone call away from bailing her sister out.

My phone vibrates again. Another Mom call. Jesus.

And then, it pulls up. A jet black limo from one of the better limo rental places. Scrubbed whitewalls, gleaming rims. It's got to be the ride of the King and Queen. He gets out, Nick does, that Ichabod-skinny lacrosse captain, and, sure as shit, the delicate, bracelet-covered arm of Martha follows. It's like they've practiced this. A red carpet entrance paparazzi-ready. Her gown is amazing. Salmon, strapless organza. There's a crisscross bodice and a little rose at the waist. The skirt is full and reaches just below her knees. Martha has great calves. Slender, long. I must have sighed, or even gasped, really loud, because Connor nudges me. "I'll ask you again. Seen enough?"

I nod, but keep staring at them, *Marnick*, as they saunter into Prom.

Bitch, says Sabine.

"No kidding," I say, out loud.

"Huh?" says Connor.

Mom calls me a third time. I slide the answer slide and hiss, "What?"

There is quiet on the line.

"Mom?"

I look up at Connor, whose eyebrows are squinching again. I shake the phone, as if it'll correct a bad connection. Why won't she talk?

Then, her breath, exhaling around a raspy, throat. An after-weeping noise. The sound of fear that you just don't hear come out of my mother. "Brady, honey, your dad's in the hospital. There's been an accident."

twenty-three

St. Vincent's Medical Center is the hospital where Sabine and I were born. It's also the hospital where Sabine's body was hauled for organ harvest after the accident. Now, it's where Dad is hooked up to monitors behind a curtained slice of hospital room. Not only was he in a car accident, but apparently suffered a heart attack as well.

Connor had dropped me off in front of the hospital, his face stiff with fear, but trying to look hopeful. "This is the best heart place on the West Coast," he said. "Your dad will be fine."

Inside my own heart was squeezed, having its own attack. My father, the minor league ball player. The Nike executive. The strongest man I knew. How could his body fail him? Who would dare to run into him after all he's been through? "Thanks," I said, shaking, and trying so hard not to explode into a zillion fragments. "I'll call you. OK?"

Connor moved in to hug me, but I couldn't do it. It was like my entire body had been flattened—a freezer bag before you seal it up. I had nothing. And what I did have, I needed to fold and tuck somewhere safe. Instead of hugging Connor back, I hugged myself as I scrambled out the truck and into the well-lit building of miracles.

* * *

Mom is in the waiting room area making calls, and she opens her free arm, guiding me in an awkward embrace. "I'll call you Ma, soon as I know anything."

She gets off the phone and has me sit down next to her on the hard foam seat cushions in the glassed-in visitor's lounge. Soothing aqua paint, a flat panel TV, and an intercom announcing hospital coded alerts every so often keeps us company while she unfolds the sequence of events that led to now.

A buzz of words I half understand. Hypertension, ventricular arrhythmia, myocardial infarction. And this. He'd been drinking. The car accident, running a light in his Fusion, it was his fault. He slammed into another car and thank God nobody else was hurt. "Thank God," Mom says, and as though conjuring her inner Nona, she makes the sign of the cross.

"He's pretty drugged up now, Brady. But I know he'd love to see you. Can you handle it? Seeing him on a gurney all hooked up to monitors?"

I'm scared. Really freaked, but I nod, biting down hard on my lip. I don't tell Mom, but the image in my head is the one in the paper. Sabine under a tarp.

Mom puts her arm around my shoulder and together we walk down the shiny hall toward a pair of swinging doors. Cardiac Care Unit reads the marquee above them. There's a poster-sized sign to the right: TELEMETRY. ABSOLUTELY NO CELL PHONE USE. I turn mine off, and so does Mom, and the doors magically part, like we're in some James Bond world.

Inside the CCU everything revolves around the nurse's station, which is like the hole of a doughnut. The unit is arranged in a circle, with the patients spoked out in their little critical care cubicles. Dad's behind a glass wall and two sets of curtains, and I can hear him snoring as we walk in. "That's good, right? That he's asleep?"

Mom pushes me in front of her because it's too narrow for us to walk in side-by-side.

What I see before I see Dad are all the monitors and their jaggedy lines. It's like "the wave" in a stadium where people rise and fall as a group. Dad's heart. There's beeping that sounds like something's wrong, but no nurses are rushing in, so it's probably just part of the normal state of affairs.

It's dark in this micro-room, and Dad's eyes are closed. Green, black, red and yellow wires emerge from Dad's hospital gown. On his index finger there's a little clip and another wire tethering him to one of the bleeping monitors. I can see some of Dad's chest in the split his gown makes, and all his hair has been shaved off. Small suction cups hold the wires in place. Dad's covered in suction cups. I touch his hand, the one with the clip, and he quivers.

Mom whispers, "The doctors want him to rest as much as possible. Steady rhythm, they keep saying is the goal."

I jerk my hand away, thinking, I've probably already screwed up. Dad's five-o'clock shadow covers the bottom half of his face. He's a twice-a-day shave guy if the occasion calls for it. Now, he looks a little like a bum. "I love you," I whisper. "I love you so much."

Dad stays asleep the whole time we're there, and at some point in the middle of the night, Mom suggests we go home, get some shut-eye, and then return the next day.

Shut-eye. I can't imagine it. But I do as she says, and we creep home like zombies. Neither of us can talk. All we can do is look straight ahead and go forward.

Mom goes into her bedroom and clicks closed the door. I go to Sabine's room and lie on top of her rose and pink quilt next to the American Girl cheerleader doll with the grassy-green pom-poms wedged into its tiny plastic hands. It still smells perfumy in here, after all these months, but now the perfume is tinged with something else. A rotten, decomposing scent, like flower stems soaked in water too long.

I open and close my fists, like I'm squeezing invisible lemons. *Sabine, what the hell? You're supposed to be protecting us.*

Nothing.

Maybe what Nona says is true about purgatory and praying for limboed souls, lest they remain forever in a state of sin. I wonder if Sabine would have done anything differently had she known her fate. Would she have chosen Connor over Nick for real? Would she have tried less hard to be first and best in everything she did? So now, she's had to outsource her amends to her living relations. We, the Wilsons and Panapentos, have to kneel before the electric candle version of her, the image of a smiling, sweet Sabine. The image Nona and Nono want to take to their own graves.

I'm furious with her. She doesn't deserve heaven. Eternal damnation is too good for Sabine. Her father lies in a hospital bed fighting for his life because of her. Connor got kicked out of school because of her. Her beloved cheering squad fell apart after she died. Greenmeadow is now known as "that tragic school."

How did you turn into such a liar, Sabine?

Somehow, amid the questions and the anger and the sorrow, I fall asleep. A deep, hard, dreamless sleep. And when I wake up in the morning, sun blasting through Sabine's bedroom window, the first thing I notice is my hands are still covered in charcoal.

twenty-four

Dad is awake and spooning anemic custard into his mouth when Mom and I return Sunday morning. He's shaved, or been shaved, and he looks pretty much like himself. The wires are still coming out of him like Frankenstein, but his cheeks are rosy and he smiles around his spoon when we arrive.

"Little Bird," he says. "Your old man's turned into an old man, looks like."

The peaks on the heart monitor are little Mt. Hood after little Mt. Hood. I figure joking is probably on the *yes* list. "If you think I'm pushing your wheelchair, forget it."

Mom leans over his bedrail and gives him a juicy kiss, and he says, "Uh-oh, we're gonna get kicked out of here if you can't behave."

We're in there a few minutes more, making small talk, and then in comes the nurse, so we're asked to leave. It's check this, check that, bed pan, and meds. "Why don't you give us a half hour or so. Go get something from the cafeteria," the nurse suggests. "It's Mother's Day, after all. They have some strawberry crepes I hear."

Mother's Day. I completely spaced it. And I spend the next several minutes, as we're negotiating the various wings of St. Vincent's, apologizing. If Mom's upset, she doesn't show it. "No worries. Really, the last thing we need to do right now is add some obligatory Hallmark event to our schedules. You just being here, with me and your dad, is Mother's Day gift enough."

And then, after we're sitting in some orange plastic chairs with plates of semi-cooked pancakes in front of us, she stirs her cup of hospital coffee and says, "Anyways, Mother's Day, so soon after losing a child, is like an entire country rubbing salt in your eyes. Never-the-less, we do need to pay a visit to your grandmother."

My heart takes this in two ways. First, there's the sorrow for Mom, any mom, who gets slapped across the face with constant reminders that her baby is dead. But the other way my heart hears this is a different kind of sorrow. The pity kind of sorrow. The, *What am I, chopped liver?* sorrow. *I'm your baby, too, Mom. Can you even look at me?*

I, too, am stirring and sipping crappy coffee. Lukewarm watery brown elixir. All around us are visitors. Some happy and balloon-carrying, no doubt headed to the birth wing to sneak peeks at the newborns in their lives. Some heavy-hearted, tired-eyed. Whoever they're here for is not doing well.

There are nurses and doctors and other hospital workers peppered about on the orange chairs. Expressions range from grim to jubilant. Bad news:Good news.

Cheer up, I think. *Get Cheery. Keep Cheering. Cheer.* All those variations of an uplifting word.

Mom reaches for my arm and pats it. "I'm hoping that we can just move forward from here on out. Clean, fresh slate."

Now would be the time to ask Mom. But I can't form the words. What would I say? *Mom, I know you've been cheating on Dad.* Or maybe, *Mom, does that mean you're going to break it off with whoever you've been seeing?* Instead of anything like a confrontation, I smile and nod and agree. "That'd be great."

But Mom has some confronting of her own to do. She says, "We need to talk about the company you've been keeping."

She means Connor.

"I know you have a different version of how things went down with Sabine, but, trust me. That boy is bad news."

I take in a breath, all set for a rebuttal. So many ways to prove she's wrong. Unfortunately, she's not finished yet.

"I'm not telling this to make you feel guilty, Brady, but with your dad, well, I think his worrying about you put him over the edge."

If she were aiming for a bull's-eye, she nailed it. I stir the coffee some more, and watch the liquid swirl around. Our pancakes, untouched, are congealing. The syrup mortaring them together. They look as appetizing as a brick wall.

"You have to promise me, for your father's sake, that you'll have nothing more to do with him."

The faint gray of charcoal remains on my fingers. When I close my eyes, I see yesterday's sketch. Connor's form emerging from shadows and lines. "Mom, it's gotten a bit more complicated."

I tell her about Mrs. Cupworth, and her generous offer to have me use her studio. And how Connor is now her gardener. I leave out the part that he's also my model. And how his lips feel against mine. And how Sabine used him. And how he makes me happier than anything else right now. I leave all of that out.

Mom looks up at the big shop lights in the hospital cafeteria. Searching for a solution. A next demand. What she settles on is, "I'm one-hundred percent for you and your art, Brady. But I will have to have a conversation with Mrs. Cupworth about the boy."

She can't even say his name.

She adds, "Your dad, if everything keeps improving, will be back home in a few days. But, it's up to us to provide a stress-free environment. Please understand how important that is."

*   *   *

On the way to Nona's, my heart is split kindling. I think about that last therapy session, and the way I just walked out. And the comment I made about burning Sabine, and my father's overly hard slap. The bruises and the wounds. The fractures and pain. I think about Nona's beliefs: the way to salvation is prayer, sacrifice, virtue. Saint Agatha would see her breasts sliced off her chest rather than allow a man to have her. The Nicene Creed's way to Heaven: We believe in one holy Catholic and apostolic Church. We acknowledge one baptism for the forgiveness of sins. We look for the resurrection of the dead, and the life of the world to come. Amen.

There is nothing about truth in the creed, only faith. Maybe faith is what's important. Truth just gets in the way. Maybe shoving truth down everyone's throats is only a way to invite more pain into your life. At the end of the day, maybe the story of how Sabine died, at the hands of a reckless stoner, maybe that's the right answer. Maybe that's the tale that goes down in history because it's the one that works. Dad's heart will heal. My heart? Well, I'm young.

We carry a bag of poppy seed bagels, cream cheese, sliced salmon, tomatoes and red onions into the pink aluminum house. I'm holding a fistful of irises wrapped in dark green tissue. My grandparents are in their easy chairs watching an old Doris Day movie, terrycloth towels draped over the headrests of their La-Z-Boys, to absorb the grease from their scalps. It's one of the things that pains Mom to see, these hints of dying dignity, but, as she says, old age has its own set of priorities.

"Oh, Sonia, with all the worries, you didn't need to do this." Nona says, but anyone can see, she's really happy to see us. "How is he, John?"

"Lucky, actually," says Mom. "It's too soon to tell how

much heart muscle was damaged, but he's stable and the doctor thinks he has a good chance at a full recovery."

Nono turns off the overly loud TV, and calls from the adjoining room. "Does he have a good heart man working on him?"

Doctors with specialties are all "men" with Nono. You don't see a dermatologist, it's a skin man. And if there's something wrong with your knees or your hips, you see a bone man.

"St. Vinnie's is the best place on the West Coast for the heart," Mom says, echoing Connor's assurances.

Mom doesn't mention anything about the drunk driving, and it occurs to me that Dad's heart attack will be the story we spin. The booze didn't cause the accident, a stressed-out heart did. A wave of sadness bowls me over because I understand, for Dad's sake, why this half-lie must be woven into our fabric, joining all the other lies that are thick as a shawl now. How easy it seems to be to tell yourself the story you want to hear. Dad was a victim, not the cause of his situation. Just like Sabine.

"Well, happy Mother's Day, Ma," says Mom.

I hand Nona the flowers, and she makes a fuss. Then directs me to run water into one of the fourteen cut-crystal vases she keeps in the curio. "You don't look so good, *Nipote*," she says.

The fact that I've had three hours of sleep and my heart broken, well, that might have something to do with it. *Maybe you should get your own heart man*, says Sabine, making a rare appearance, her first since Dad's heart attack.

I want to tell my dead sister to leave me alone. You got your way. I'll keep your secret.

Nona suggests we all eat the bagels and have some iced tea, so we sit down at the Formica table, Nono abandoning his La-Z-Boy, but looking longingly over at it every few minutes.

Mom is trying to lighten things up over brunch, and she brings up Mrs. Cupworth and her generosity. "Brady really must have impressed that woman," she says.

"That the society lady at the Art Night? The one who made the principal look like he saw a ghost when she got up there and pointed her finger? She bought our Brady's picture?"

"She's a huge supporter of the arts. This thing she's doing, it's not just for me. She wants to make the studio space available continually."

"Nono and I gotta fill out the ballots," she says, reminded about the arts funding initiative. "The election. I don't know who to vote for. It's this idiot or the other idiot."

Our bagel brunch goes on like this. Normal Nona and Nono blather. They go from the election to the takeover of the bagel store by a bigger bagel store to echoing Mrs. Cupworth, whether or not it's warm enough to plant tomatoes, and then, finally, we talk about Dad's heart attack. And Dad and Mom.

"We've had our problems, but in a weird way, this crisis has served as a wakeup call for us. We're committed to working things out. And getting Brady back on track."

Getting Brady back on track?

As if she's reading my mind, Nona says, "I didn't think our little *Nipote* was off the track, Sonia. Look what she had to deal with."

Nono adds, "She's smart girl. She'll be fine." Then he reaches over and pinches my cheek with his overgrown, thick fingernails.

"You don't know everything, Ma," Mom continues. "About Brady."

Sabine's electric candle is unplugged in the next room. St. Agatha is withholding judgment.

Nona says, "What I know is our Brady is a special girl. Her heart is full of life. You and John, you raised a good girl."

"Amen," says Nono.

Mom nods and dabs at some fallen poppy seeds with her index finger. "Yes, she's smart. And good. But the world is a different place now. The drugs in the school. The casual sex. Navigating a girl through that—it's one landmine after another."

I am tired of being talked about as though I'm not in the room. "Drugs? I don't do drugs. And I don't have, uh, casual sex."

"Of course you don't, *Nipote*," says Nono, squeezing my cheek again.

"It's not you I don't trust," says Mom.

"Boys are boys, Brady," adds Nona.

"Connor's not like that," I blurt. "In fact, Sabine? She had Nick believing that she and Connor were fooling around, just to get him jealous. If ever there was a girl you should have *navigated*, well, it wasn't me."

President Kennedy glares at me from the wall. Sabine says, *Thanks a lot, Midge.*

So there it is. I'm that fallen apostle called out on canvas in Da Vinci's *The Last Supper*. Judas, skulking in his green and blue robes, clutching the bag of money. I put a hand over my mouth because I know the next thing that comes out will be about Dad's drinking.

And all around the table, our own last supper, our brunch, is silence.

Finally, Mom calmly gets up and starts clearing the table. I get up too. It is Mother's Day, after all. Wordlessly, we scrape, rinse, wash, and dry. Wrap up the leftover bagels. Nona and Nono go back to their Doris Day movie. It's not the *Que Sera Sera* flick, but one just as adorable.

When we are done, we offer them kisses and promise to call with updates about Dad. The whole ride back to our house, Mom says nothing. But after we get in the house, and she's had a chance to call Dad and talk to the doctor, she sits me down at the edge of her bed. For the first time, I see lines around her eyes and mouth. A little gray around her hairline. I'm seeing, in Mom, the old lady she will one day be, and my heart aches for her. She puts an arm around me, and guides my chin so we're looking eye to eye. She says, "Sometimes love takes a wrong turn, Brady. I've taken a wrong turn here and there in the name of love. I want to spare you that pain. You're my daughter, and I want you to skip right over the heartaches and go directly to the right choice."

Her dark Panapento eyes. Her eyebrows tweezed just so. She says, "That's not fair of me, I realize. You have to make mistakes in order to grow. But I'm begging you. Pleading with you. Do not fall in that murky well right now. Not now."

twenty-five

The Monday after Prom is always a waste. Hungover students. The fallout of whatever breakups or hookups went down. Good luck to Pale Blue Dot or any of them who think actual educating will happen.

First thing, before trig even, Martha finds me and she's holding a yellow rose. A perfect yellow rose. "I am so sorry to hear about your dad, Brady," she says, offering the flower to me. Plus a card.

My throat is dry but I manage a gracious *Thank you*. I say, "He's expected to make a full recovery," in my robot voice.

But then, behind her happy, happy Princess face, there's a little wrinkle. Something not quite right.

"He is," I insist. "Going to be fine."

"It's not that," she says, continuing to thrust the rose my way until I take it from her. "It's just, well, Nick told me that you're involved with Connor."

"Involved? Well, not involved, really," I stammer, sort of Judas-like.

"And that he's been filling your head with a bunch of lies."

Nick. Of course he'd be doing his best to save his hide now that he knows what I know.

"Martha, I realize that you're hot on Nick and all, but, he's got a dark side. He's guilty of more than you think."

"Guilty of what? You mean loving a girl who cheated on him? Repeatedly?"

I can't believe it. Nick's spreading who-knows-what sort of crap about Connor. I reach my rose-wielding hand toward Martha, but she steps back, like I'm about to strike her.

"I don't know what Nick told you, Martha, but it's not true. And, as far as the Connor thing. I'm not involved with him. Not anymore, anyway."

As soon as they're out of my mouth, those words *not anymore*, a huge cavern tears open inside of me.

Martha, though, she bounces up like a happy Jack-in-the-box. "So, you came to your senses, then? About Connor? I'm so happy to hear that."

Why am I even friends with this girl? The way she glows with satisfaction when the world matches up to her sense of order and the way things should be. I want to tell her that it's only temporary. Once Dad recovers, once Mom re-busies herself with her own life, I can see who I want to see. Why should Martha be the only one on the planet who gets to do whatever the hell she wants? I glare at her. "Happy? Well, good for you, Martha. I'm glad you're happy. Because I am not."

She pushes a hunk of her shiny mahogany hair back over her shoulder and grins. "Cheer up, Brady. It's time you got back into things around here. I'd love it, assuming your dad's out of the woods and everything, if you could come over later and help me with my Rose Festival Court speech. You're so good with words, you know?"

Good with words. Maybe I should show her the power of words. Let her hear Nick in all his glory.

"I'll come over, Martha, but there's a few things you need to know about that boyfriend of yours."

"Now, Brady, can't we just all be friends?" Martha's Rose Festival smile is lightning rod against any negative Nick information.

I feel trapped. And then, before I can say anything more,

she pours her Martha honey all over everything. "I've put the word out. I hope you don't mind, but there will be dinners delivered. There's a sign-up schedule on Facebook. A page, actually. It's called Johnscare. You can like it. Join it. You can write in dietary preferences."

"That's way too thoughtful, Martha," I tell her. "Really, we can manage."

"It's the least I can do. Your family means so much to me."

It hits me that the reason I resent Martha so much is that I think that sometimes she just spouts off with things. That she doesn't really mean them. Sabine says, *Not everyone's as true-hearted as you, Midge.*

I try to meet her kindness with some of my own. "Martha. You totally will get this Rose Festival Queen thing. Your name stamped into the brick. The whole deal." And she will. Because the Marthas of the world do get everything they go after.

She leans in after I say that, and she plants a tiny kiss on my cheek. A small grace.

Throughout the rest of the day, teachers are extra careful around me. The word *sorry* rains down on me like confetti. And the flowers. Since when do you give people flowers when their parents are ill? I realize that everyone's just taking Martha's lead. Even Walter Pine. Even Cathi Serge. Wilted rhodies, an azalea cluster. It's Brady Appreciation Day at Greenmeadow.

And Connor keeps calling and texting. I've yet to give him an update. I don't know what to say to him. He's wondering if I'll be over at Mrs. Cupworth's later. He really wants to see me. He thinks about me all the time.

My stomach is a knot the size of Blue Dot's overhead projector.

Finally, I text him back, *Have to go to hospital after school.*

Dad better.

I tap out an *xo* and then delete it. Add it back, delete it. Press send. I wish I could just be sitting in Connor's truck, next to him, the two of us leaving this world where everything is broken.

The image of Nona, the way she works a rosary, finds its way into my head. The same way that Martha pops a pill when she's upset, Nona says a Hail Mary. It occurs to me that when people feel powerless to change the way things are, they try and find some sort of magic. Something they can grab quickly, and believe in. I don't have that. Maybe that's my problem.

It turns out that I'm not going to the hospital after all because Dad's going to some sort of recovery outpatient thing. It's unclear whether this has to do with his heart or his drinking problem, and Mom is keeping it unclear. It's exactly the sort of thing I wish I could talk to Connor about. Family secrets, all the craziness at home. But I'm forbidden to see Connor, so where I am going, for reasons I can't quite explain to myself, is Martha's house. To help her with her Rose Festival Court speech.

Martha's house is almost as grand as Mrs. Cupworth's, but much less formal. There's that pair of mastiffs that lope about. Some exotic birds that screech. Despite the full time staff, the house has a very lived-in feel. Older, worn furniture, scuffed up by pets. They're wealthy, but total Democrats, the Hornbuckles. Evidence of their foundation associations is everywhere. Handmade Guatemalan rugs made by marginalized mountain women dot their floors. Plaques are hung askew here and there: MAC Club Tennis Task Force donor, Leukemia Society Sponsor, Healthy Rivers and Streams Coordinator. It's like the Do-Gooder Museum at Martha's.

Clearly, Martha is the Do-Gooder in training.

Right away, no sooner am I in the house, when she starts rehearsing. "My topic is on introducing free range poultry to foodservice in the Oregon schools."

"Nice," I say, following Martha into the library, where there's a podium and microphone set up.

Martha goes through her speech a half-dozen times, and I'm not being a good listener. I'm distracted, wondering if Connor's up the street, or at Mrs. Cupworth's, or in Forest Park. I've plastered an attentive smile on, my eyes don't leave the podium, but, truly, I haven't heard a word. So when Martha says, "Brady? Brady? Should I go into the hand-eviscerating part or is that TMI?" I snap to attention.

"Hand-eviscerating?"

I'm spared from critical input though, because just then, in walks Nick. It must be one of his few lacrosse-free days, because he's wearing civilian clothes. An Abercrombie tee-shirt and jeans. Some Day-Glo kicks and his usual indoor-outdoor sunglasses. "Brady," he says after kissing Martha on the top of her head the way fathers often do. "What are you doing here? Shouldn't you be at your dad's bedside?"

"Nick. Really." Martha starts apologizing for her rude boyfriend.

I hold up my hand. "Not a problem. I have known for a while that tact and manners are not Nick's strong suit."

"Speaking of manners," Nick says, peeking over his shades for effect. Leveling his gaze. "We saw you and that creepy pal of yours spying on us at Prom. No wonder your Dad had a heart attack. His living daughter hanging out with the guy who killed his dead one."

Martha punches Nick's arm, and under her breath half-whispers, "I can't believe you just said that."

But I can.

"You know, Martha, I really need to go," I say, grabbing my things and heading for the various rooms that will lead me, eventually, out the front door. "I'm sure Nick can help you with the hand-eviscerating stuff."

Before Martha can intervene, or sweet talk or use her world-class diplomatic skills to stop me, I've slammed the custom twelve-panel wood door behind me, and just doing that, that little act of movement and closure, makes me feel better. But a second later, I'm back to feeling furious again. That bastard parked my sister's Volvo right in the middle of the drive. Not even over to the side, courteously out of the way of other potential comings and goings. No, Nick is all about possession. About winning.

I run my hand along the boxy hood, the familiar chrome door handle. It's so unfair. He should not have this car. And then, in concert with a shrieking crow in a nearby tree, it's Sabine. *You know where the key is, little sister.*

The hide-a-key. I'd forgotten until this moment that Sabine was always getting locked out of her car, and she had run out of AAA allowances for Slim Jim assistance. Dad put a magnetic box under her car, near the driver's side wheel. Like the sneaky spy I've just been accused of being, I drop to my knees, reach under, and, sure enough.

I think about how easy it would be to just take the car. Drive down the gated Hornbuckle driveway, and leave nothing but tires tracks. Imagining Nick's face upon discovering the missing car is almost good enough. But then I think of Dad, and the last thing I want to do is create more stress. How would I explain stealing the car?

So I pocket the key and keep walking. A small piece of Sabine's property, that's all I have left. But, somehow, for today anyway, it's enough.

*   *   *

Once I'm off the Hornbuckle compound, past the tree house where Martha and I smoked our first joint a few years ago, my body wants to head right. Up the hill. To the house where, a year ago, they had an auction to raise money for a cheerleading team that no longer exists. Where a few months ago, a girl sought help to pull a car—once belonging to her sister and now commandeered by a maniac—out of a ditch. Where a month ago a girl tried to kiss a boy who didn't kiss her back. A boy who is baffled by the sudden cold shoulder given him by the girl, who just a few days ago, spent an afternoon studying and reproducing the lines and angles that made her bones turn to jelly.

I turn the Volvo key over and over in my hand. I owe him an explanation. At least that.

I knock lightly, hoping, praying, even, that Connor will not open the door. Maybe his mother, the interior designer, will be home. She'll look confused that I'm here, but she'll be gracious, and invite me in for tea and ask how my family is doing, and she'll go white with shock when she hears my father just had a heart attack. *But he's expected to make a full recovery*, I'll sing-song.

I'm still lost in the imaginary conversation with Connor's mother when he rips the door open wide. In one second I can tell, he's completely baked.

"You sure you should be here?" he says, the smell of weed wafting out his lips.

All that comes out of my mouth are swear words. "Shit, Connor, what the fuck?" Though I'm here to explain why I can't see him for a while, I'm derailed by the fact that he's high. I feel, somehow, invested in his poor choices. Dr. Stern would call that the slippery slope of co-dependence.

Before I can even utter a word, he cuts in with, "Sounds like your mom put a bug in Lilith Cupworth's ear. Guess she must have shaken the old lady up because she started talking about restraining orders and whatnot."

An elevator feeling slips into my body. Guilt. Fear. A mixture of emotions. *Mom.* Jesus. "Connor, that really sucks. I'll set her straight about you. But, you're going to get kicked out of your house if you're not careful. Is that what you want? For your mom to send you off to live with your dad in some trailer park?"

Connor shrugs. "My life is shit here. People think what they think, and that's not going to change. It was super lame of me to get close to you, anyway. Given what we were up against. It'll be better, me living a mountain range away from all this crap."

When he says "all this crap," I feel like he just slapped me in the face, giving me a shiner worse than Dad's. Only this bruise won't disappear in a few days. I want to blink back time. Go back to the day before Dad's accident. Or, as long as we're in a time machine, go back to the day before Sabine's accident. Everything is unraveling, and this boy who is the center of it all, he's just one big, snagged thread. "Connor, believe me, I wish there was another way. I wish we could just figure this out, but right now, I need to help put my family back together."

"Yeah," he says, his eyes red and itchy looking, "well, like your sister always said, 'People love winners. As for losers, they might as well burn in hell.'"

I notice that there's no earring dangling from his lobe as he shuts the door, giving me one last look at a long slice of him—a boy who once held my sister's future in his hand.

twenty-six

I walk through the next few weeks like a painting of myself. Something formed by someone else. I'm viewing this painting as an outsider, too. Watching myself going through the motions. Brushing, flossing, taking out the trash. In trig, I get my first A. My paper on Flannery O'Connor is a solid B, but Mrs. McConnell tells me I can do better. *Where's the passion?* she writes on my paper all red inked and loopy.

Passion? I'm done with that. I've joined the rosary prayer people. The pill-poppers. Like a Nike ad, I'm "just do it-ing" my way through life. Every time I think about Connor, how much I miss him, I flip a switch in my heart. Better to just move forward. Don't feel. Don't feel. Don't feel.

Dad is released. He's on a strict no cholesterol, low salt, 1500-calorie diet. He has to go to meetings and talk about one day at a time. Mom has turned into his personal cheerleader. She follows his diet to the letter. She buys a kitchen scale and, no kidding, she's weighing lettuce leaves. She dumps all the whiskey down the drain. She's counting out raisins for his oatmeal. Dad can't return to work for another month, so afternoons, it's me and Dad on the couch, watching *Wheel of Fortune* and *World Series of Poker*. The occasional Mariner's game.

He's always asking me if I'm happy. "You seem down, Little Bird," he'll say.

"I'm not," I argue. "I'm fine."

"I am really ashamed, Brady. So ashamed." I know he's

thinking about when he slapped me, but when he tells he wants to make amends for everything, who I think about is Connor. The person who should be forgiven more than anyone. I want to tell Dad everything I know. About Connor, about Sabine. About Nick. But Dad's so broken. So fragile.

I pat his hand. On TV, a Versace-wearing poker player who reminds me of Nick slowly chews gum. I hope he loses all his money.

Dad says, "Are you sure? Are you sure you're fine?"

I nod. *Fine.* Stupid word. A word that's empty of feeling. The perfect word for now.

Don't feel, Brady. Just don't.

And in the real world. The world that continues on, the ballot measure passes. Arts and electives are safe for another year. Bowerman and McConnell get to teach their classes again. Pink slips are tucked back into the district file cabinet. Everybody cheer.

A couple times a week, I head up to Mrs. Cupworth's and work on some sketches, and even a few paintings. At first, after she fired Connor, I wanted to boycott the whole artist-in-residence thing. Let her know she'd drawn a line in the sand. Mom and I had it out about that.

"I'm sorry but I had to tell her," Mom said. "I let her come to her own decision, but I had to give her the facts."

"What facts, Mom? You don't know the facts."

In my new life as a robot, I decided to go back to Mrs. Cupworth's studio. Pretend to still be an artist. Fake it 'til I make it. I set up a still life with a St. Agatha statue and a bowl of plastic apples that I got from Michael's. I printed out a version of da Vinci's The Last Supper from Wikipedia, and blew it up at a copy store. It's scary pixelated, and I set it behind the bowl of apples and the St. Agatha, so it really just looks like colorful embroidery. At least that's what shows up on my canvas when I dab my brush into color after color. Art, reduced to upholstery. That's sort of how I feel.

The sketch I did of Connor, the day Dad had his heart attack, I can't bring myself to throw it out, or refine it. I simply tuck it into the sketchpad where I imagine it'll smear itself unrecognizable. I think about him every day. And then I make myself unthink about him. But I can't help it. Every tree on this property, the shrubs, the roses—which are now being tended by Mrs. Cupworth's entourage of gardeners—remind me of Connor. His lips and the dimple at the side of his mouth. Is there no end to grieving? Every time you love someone, it seems, you're setting yourself up for a fall. Sabine isn't the only one who took a chance and lost.

"Don't feel. Don't feel." I yell at myself out loud one day, just as Lilith Cupworth sashays through the door.

"Don't feel what?" she says, eagerly peering over the canvas.

"Stop messing up the painting, I guess," I tell her.

"Doesn't look very messy to me," she says, appraising it with a bit of a sigh in her voice.

I step back a bit, squinch my eyes the way I'd seen Connor do a million times. "Do you like it?"

She sighs again. "I do. I like it." And then she stares square into my face. "It's perfectly fine. But, to be honest, it doesn't quite have your energy behind it. It lacks a certain … oh, I don't know. Authority?"

"Passion, you mean?" I fill in the party line.

"Right."

I bite my lip.

"Brady, Dear. I know you miss that boy. I know a broken heart when I see one."

I want to tell her she's wrong. She can't see the shards of my broken heart. I've swept them up. And, I want to spill all the other things she can't possibly see, about Mom and Sabine and Dad and the web of lies, but, truly, I don't see the point.

"The two of you were quite adorable together, no denying that. But. I've seen what drugs can do. Seen it in my own children. Cocaine. Marijuana. You can't trust a drug addict, you know."

Cocaine? Where did that idea come from?

"Mrs. Cupworth, it wasn't about drugs. That's not why my mother intervened."

"No? Well, she was clearly very worried for your safety. She told me that the young man was high when he caused the accident that killed your dear sister."

I take in a deep breath, and hear a ringing sound in my ears. It's like the way Nona always described the trumpets of Heaven, only, for me the ringing is more like a Greek chorus chanting *He was high when he killed her!* over and over and over. Duplicity, I think. Double standard. And then, I just say it. Plain and simple. "Connor Christopher was not high when Sabine plunged to her death. That's what nobody will believe. My sister performed a move that was well outside of her abilities. She wanted to win, and she pushed the envelope into crazy. She was the one who made the mistake, not Connor. She had secrets. She was—"

I can't finish my sentence. Mrs. Cupworth is clutching the strand of pearls that hangs just below her throat. "What, child, she was what?"

"She was a liar," I shout. "She was the one who shouldn't have been trusted. She and her so-called boyfriend were playing an ugly, dark game with each other. Connor just got caught in the middle."

I go on to explain The Eraser Game that Sabine used to play. "It was like that, only instead of scarring up a forearm, it was other people's lives."

Mrs. Cupworth shakes her head. "These are certainly odd times, Brady."

"Well," I tell her, "I guess you should know what you're in for if you want to open your house up to teenagers from Greenmeadow."

All the way back down the hill to my house, I think about what I said. Regret and shame and anger all mixed up together like Nona's sauce. I'm wondering if that's why Catholics trot off to confession every Saturday afternoon like clockwork. It would be so nice to walk into Holy Redeemer's darkened space, wait in the line of sinners, and pop into the booth to spill my troubles. My guilt over betraying Sabine. Like Beaverton Grief & Family but instead of a middle aged shrink with dandruff and yapping mutts next door, you get some Angel of God who stays on his side of the panel, and gives you a little homework assignment that you can punch out in a few minutes.

For no apparent reason, Natalie jumps into my thoughts. There was that day, late in the summer of Johnsaffair, Sabine painted rubber cement all over Natalie's golf club handles. Dad was furious. His Scottish temper making his face redder than a sinking sun, he demanded that we apologize to Natalie, and pay for cleaning and re-gripping the clubs. I didn't even know what had happened, but I silently took the blame and punishment right alongside my sister.

Afterwards, depleted of a year's worth of babysitting money, Sabine was jubilant. She knew this stunt was the last straw. And sure enough, by the next weekend, Johnsaffair was history.

Her apology was not sincere—it was just for show. She'd do it again in a minute, she told me, as Natalie's Pathfinder barreled down Pelican Lane for the last time.

A few late lilacs still offer some pleasant scent as I cut through the dog park near home. It's warm and drizzly out. Typical Rose Festival weather. Summer's coming on fast, which always makes me sad for some reason. Maybe it's the way a mother feels when her baby learns to walk, or gets a tooth. That sense of fleeting time. Life moving ahead on its own terms. The brand new bright green leaves have matured, and they're getting rubbery. Apple blossoms are gone, and hard, golf ball-sized fruit dots the trees. Dreams turning into wakeful realities. A next thing and a next and a next. But never a straight line. Never life just getting better and easier. Everything has a cost. I suppose I'm done protecting my sister. I suppose I'm ready to face the consequences of that.

Why now? says Sabine.

I'm still a few blocks from home when Martha calls, all breathless and in a tizzy. Tomorrow is coronation day, where she and the other princesses will gather in the Veteran's Memorial Coliseum and, in front of an enthusiastic $30-a-ticket crowd, a Rose Festival Queen will be announced. The lucky Princess who becomes Queen has her lowly court tiara replaced with a queen tiara by one of the ancient Rosarians while the other princesses pretend to be happy for her. Poise under pressure, Martha tells me, is one of the things they've been drilling into them. Martha is pretty sure she's neck-and-neck with Cleveland High School's Princess. A girl who recently donated some of her bone marrow stem cells to a leukemia patient. "But her GPA is only 2.9," Martha says, hopefully, over the phone.

"Maybe you should offer someone a kidney or something," I tell her. "It's not too late, is it?"

"Will you come?" she wants to know. "I'll pay for your ticket. It would be so great to see you in the audience."

I think about it for a minute. Sitting there in the cold venue, where people go to see monster trucks and hockey games. It's the closest thing Portland has to a beauty contest, this Rose Festival Court gala. "Will Nick be there?" I ask.

"Oh Brady, don't be like that. I want you both there. Can't you just get over your issues with one another?"

I don't want to give her an ultimatum—one of those him or me deals—but it seems that Martha needs all the facts about this boyfriend of hers. She needs to know what he's capable of. "Can you come over? There's something you should hear."

Martha shows up bearing a platter of low-fat, tofu spring rolls. And a six-pack of Evian. "They say spring water is good for the heart," she tells us.

Dad is happy to see her, and Mom asks her to sit down and catch up. Martha is so good at doing the bread-and-butter thing. She launches into her free-range chicken speech, and my parents smile and nod, attentively. They wish her luck and thank her for all she's done, and then, finally, I have an opportunity to nab her and pull her into Sabine's room.

"Wow," she says, stroking Nona's rose and pink quilt. "I still can't really believe it, you know?"

I'm shaking. This is going to be harder than I thought. I grab the little cheerleader doll and start pulling at the cellophane pom-pom strips. *She loves me, she loves me not.*

"So, what is it? What do you have for me?"

I gesture toward the top of Sabine's tidy dresser next to the photo of Sabine and Martha French-braiding my hair, and point to my sister's phone. I tell Martha the code, and ask her to listen to the voicemail sequence under LoverBoy.

She takes the little techno-brick in her hand, turns it over a couple of times and says, "Isn't this a breach of privacy?" She says privacy the way Brits do, with the short-voweled *i*.

"There's a lot of breach, Martha. One could say these last

few months have been nothing *but* breach. Seriously, it's up to you, but if it were me? I'd want to know."

Martha sighs, reaches into her pocket for a pill, and swallows it with a big gulp of Evian, then drags her index finger along the bar. She puts the phone to her ear.

I yank at the little green pom-pom strips.

Martha's face goes through a spectrum of movement. First, it's all poise under pressure, but as she engages the history of Nick's messages, drilling down the conversation, poise abandons Martha. And in the end, once the cheerleader doll is holding a bald pom-pom, I'm cradling Martha in my arms. Stroking her glossy princess hair while she sops the front of my tee-shirt with her tears. This same Martha who was once a little girl who got teased for wearing *Finding Nemo* underpants. My dear friend, who frustrates, annoys and fascinates me. The girl who seems like she has all the answers, but really, is just as mixed up as the rest of us. The candidate for Queen of Rosaria whimpers into my chest, "I had no idea." She blubbers. "Why didn't she tell me?"

twenty-seven

Mom, Dad and I sit in our pricey Rose Festival Queen Coronation seats, and in front of us, in a semi-circle up on the stage, is a wave of pink. The princesses are ethnically diverse, but they are all sisters today in matching gowns, each of them delicately arranged on a chair, sparkly silver tiaras nestled upon their royal coifs.

Nick is nowhere to be seen. This morning I helped Martha apply gobs of concealer, rubbing out the black circles under her eyes. Years of charcoal shading has given me a terrific skillset. If I don't make it as an artist, there's always a career in makeup.

"He didn't take it very well," she told me.

"But, you told him what you heard, right?"

Martha assured me. It's over. Nick is history.

Now, gazing upon her calm face, her perfect smile, you'd never know she just broke up with her boyfriend. Of course, the pill she popped probably helped.

I tell myself to calm down. Enjoy the outing with my parents. Aside from his mandatory Alcoholics Anonymous meetings, it's Dad's first public event since his heart attack, and, twenty pounds slimmer, sober and well-rested, he looks like the handsome old dad of years ago. Mom and he are holding hands like a new couple. For the moment, I'm thinking, everything is perfect.

A Rosarian, dressed in a dashing red tuxedo, takes the

podium and talks about how each of these girls is an example to young people everywhere. They are the future of our city. Even though there's only one girl who will be crowned Queen, they are all winners.

Bullshit, says Sabine. Sabine, who earlier told me to pocket the key to her car. Now, my fingers reach down into the pocket of my raincoat and dig the metal notches into my skin.

A few more speeches, a list of donors and sponsors, a plug for Pacific Power.

Then, the moment we've all been waiting for.

"All princesses please stand."

The pink wave rises. I grab Dad's hand.

A disembodied announcer's voice booms out the echoey loudspeaker.

"It is my pleasure. To introduce. This year's Rose Festival Queen…"

The princesses are rapt. Trying to look poised, because the close-up cameras are zeroing in. God forbid you scowl when your name isn't the one bouncing off the coliseum walls.

"…Martha Hornbuckle."

Dad pumps his fist in the air. Mom stands and claps so loud you'd think Martha was her own daughter. And me? I'm happy in a quieter way. A fairy-tale ending way. Martha is Cinderella up there, without Prince Charming, but with all the riches and treasures.

Good for her, says Sabine, meaning it.

The Jumbotron hanging from the center of the coliseum zooms in on a little African American boy in a white suit. He holds a jeweled crown on a pillow and walks slowly, carefully to Martha, who, at this moment, is being draped in a long robe.

The camera pans to Martha, whose hands are completely covering her face while her shoulders shudder, the appropriate moment for tears, but I know those tears are not just because she won. Everyone's eyes are on the Jumbotron, or on Martha, or on the loser princesses who are graciously hugging their sister, the Queen. Maybe it's Sabine's voice that tells me to look off to the side. Maybe it's instinct, but I know that nobody else sees him at the edge of the curtained-off area dressed in his own white tux and top hat. His cocky, arms-folded posture. His gangly Ichabod Crane self. And even without the benefit of a high-tech camera, even with my regular eyes, I can tell he's been drinking. A lot. There's no doubt in my mind what he's planning.

"I'll meet you at home?" I tell my parents before dashing out to the aisle and scrambling up the stairs and out the main entrance. The only problem? I have no idea where Nick parked the Volvo. It could be anywhere. One of four parking garages or the latecomers lots that charge $20 for the benefit of an easy exit.

It's raining pretty hard, and as I wander up and down the main drag in Sabine's platform sandals looking for any glimpse of the Volvo, cars are splashing through puddles, drenching my legs and feet. My hair is the coat of a wet dog. Mascara is runny down my cheeks; I see drips of black rolling off my chin. I circle back toward the Coliseum, and teems of people are now leaving the building. I'm a salmon swimming against the current. I text Martha, *Please let me know you're ok. Saw Nick.*

But, I know it's fruitless. The princesses are banned from having their phones anywhere near the ceremony.

Maybe I should let security know, I think. Maybe I should alert Martha's parents. Maybe Nick just wanted to watch. A zillion possibilities are slamming through my head. I decide to go back into the building and head for security, but just as I'm rounding the corner to the back entrance, I catch a glimpse of a white tux and a flash of pink chiffon. The sparkle of jewels. Two figures swimming through the crowd, which then parts with *ooh*ing and *ahh*ing. When I fight my way forward, I notice that he's carrying her. Camera phones raised overhead. They think this is part of the show.

Martha is out of it. How many pills did she take to get her through this day? And then I remember Sabine telling me about the night she lost her virginity. Nick gave her something to relax. Who knows what Martha had in her little box of pills? Xanax? Ruffies?

As I fight my way through the jumble of people that stands between me and them, I realize that I need to call Connor. Now. Connor is the one person Martha and I both need on the team. Standing beside one of the Rose Quarter fountains while thunder claps and rain pelts, as Martha and Nick grow into a vague blur, I take in a deep breath and press in the number I'd recently deleted from my "favorites" list. In a gush of words, none of them "sorry," I recount the sequence of events.

"Where are you?" is all he asks.

I meet Connor across the Broadway Bridge, on the other side of Rose Festival traffic. There are no yard tools in the back of his stepfather's pickup, but there are lots of boxes.

"I'm moving," he says. "To Bend. Today, actually."

I take that in, swallow my disgust for myself. The smell of him, the feel of his body in the bench seat next to me. Why didn't I put up more of a fight? There was plenty I could have done to change that outcome, but it's too late now.

"Where do you think he took her?"

In my head I've been pondering that very question. "I think it depends on what he's after," I say. "Clearly, it's not forgiveness."

We rumble through The Pearl, all the high-end cafes and

boutiques, everything so clean and new. Connor's wipers are on super-fast, and I'm soaked to the bone. The jumble of thoughts I have range from fear for Martha to joy that I'm with Connor to worry that, once again, I'm setting myself up for disaster. "I think he's off his rocker. I mean, kidnapping the Rose Festival Queen?"

"Does anyone else know she broke up with him?"

"I doubt it," I say. "She wanted everything to be perfect today. Keeping up appearances and all that. People probably think the dramatic carting off by the prince was a new Rose Festival act."

Sabine intervenes. A matter-of-fact statement. *He drugged her.*

"Oh my God."

"What?"

Any embarrassment I feel for what I'm about to say vanishes in the face of a certain realization. "Well, Martha is famous for her pity hand jobs, right? And, occasionally, other favors? But I'm pretty damn sure she's still a virgin."

Connor's eyebrows squinch. Oh, how I've missed them.

I set him straight, pointing up toward the vast hill of green ahead of us. "He's taking her to the Witch's House."

Connor navigates the pickup through the narrow, convoluted, one-way streets near Lower Macleay Park, and surprisingly, when we get to the tiny circular parking lot, there's not one car there. Not even the Volvo.

"Any other ideas?"

I know he's up there. I don't know how I know, but I do. "The top lot," I tell Connor. "By Audubon."

We turn around, the rain still coming down in buckets, and wind up the steep streets of Northwest Portland. When we pull off Cornell and into the lot, my heart is beating as fast as the wiper blades. It's there. Sabine's Volvo. A single car in a lot usually overflowing with hikers and picnickers. Then, I see why. There's yellow caution tape crisscrossing the trail. A corrugated sign that reads, *Hazardous conditions. Trail closed.*

"Now what?" says Connor.

"I guess we go rescue the Queen," I tell him.

I reveal the key I've squirreled away, and we quickly sort out a plan. Connor will head to the Witch's House from the top, and I'll drive the Volvo back down to the Macleay entrance, and hike up from the bottom. "Are you sure?" he says, as I climb into my sister's car.

Connor's familiar face. His eyebrows and his lips. The perfectness of him. "We have to hurry," I say.

I watch him hop over the tape and disappear down the trail, and then I peel out of the gravel lot, the way I'd seen Sabine do a zillion times.

It takes forever to get back down there, the line of cars at the stop signs, pedestrians and their umbrellas and covered baby strollers. I'm prickly and hot with anxiety. When a dog-walker stops in the middle of an intersection to adjust her umbrella, I finally understand road rage. I narrowly miss the back end of the retriever at the end of her leash as I barrel by.

Still, nobody in the lower lot. A torrential downpour is blasting our fair city as it does intermittently throughout Rose Festival each year. The Volvo's wipers are old and crumbly, and I can barely see as I guide the car to a stop. I'm flinging myself out the door, when—*Take me with you.*

It's clear as day, that voice. Like she's standing next to me, whispering in my ear. *Brady, take me with you.*

Before tearing up the trail, I reach under the passenger seat, grab the Ziploc filled with Sabine, and slip it into my coat pocket. Dad, so out of it with grief and whiskey, he forgot he'd left her here. And Nick is apparently not as thorough a detailer as he fancies himself.

The bottom part of the trail is paved. Disability Access, reads a copper plaque on a rock, and by the time I'm past the paved part, where more yellow tape and hazard signs announce the closure of the trail, I realize that there's blood in drops behind me. I've been running in Sabine's platform sandals, and I've cut two nasty gashes into my feet. I keep running; the burning and aching just make me run faster. Maybe that's what St. Agatha thought as the knife severed her breasts. The bloody holes in her chest, nothing but fuel for her mission. This must be it then, the way people are guided by faith. Feeling everything, all the pain, all the fear, and continuing on.

My phone announces a text. Connor. *Hurry.*

The trail is blocked by a mudslide, and I scramble over it, one of my sandals coming loose and slipping down the bank and into the river below. I kick the other one off, too, and keep moving, running barefoot up and up. Now the trail is undercut and no wider than my hand in places, and I grab onto ferns and roots to keep from falling.

Climbing the last uphill section, around a corner, I lose my footing, and in one desperate grab, I clutch some ivy, the scourge of the park and the fir trees. Ivy that the industrious boy scouts somehow missed. Thank God. It's the only thing that keeps me from falling the height of an old growth fir, to the rocky creek below.

And then, I hear Connor's voice. And Nick. I'm running as fast as I can. My heart in my throat, out of breath, blood streaming off my feet, my raincoat flapping against my calves and the rain continually coating every mud-sliding step. Connor's voice is a quality I've never heard in him. Scared shitless, but forcing calm. "You don't want to do this," he's saying. "You really don't."

His back is toward me, Nick's is, and he's got Martha in his clutches. She's leaned over his arm like a rag doll. Her cape is gone, but she's still wearing her pink gown. The jewel-studded crown is on the ground next to her. Nick, his white tuxedo covered in mud, is holding something in his other hand. Connor can see me now and his eyes are shifting to whatever's in Nick's fist. And then I see what it is. A jagged piece of a beer bottle. He's holding it against Martha's throat. Martha, passed out and unaware that at any moment Nick could end it all.

The stone ruin, the ever-popular party and cherry-popping destination, now serves as the stage for Nick's desperate act of violence. Ferns have grown in the cracks of the stones. Blackberry vines wiggle out of the crevices like Medusa's hair. We could be on a Greek Isle somewhere, or a South American jungle, but we're not. We're still in Portland. And the contradiction of nature and humanity is strewn about all over the steps. Broken beer bottles. An empty Luncheables container. A couple of popped balloons, their latex skins littering the edge of a crumbling wall.

Nick doesn't know I'm behind him. I have one chance. I signal to Connor, my fingers forming the mouth of a shadow puppet, up, down, up, down. I want him to keep talking to distract Nick while I inch closer, furtively tip-toeing on my bloody, bare feet. *Don't fuck this up*, says Sabine.

I slowly reach into my pocket, like there's a revolver in there. And I get a big, healthy handful. Connor is telling Nick that he can help him explain what happened. And Nick just keeps saying, "You ruined everything."

And then, Sabine and me, the two of us, forever Irish twins, we take a deep, cleansing breath, and with all the strength in the world, the loudest cheer we can muster, we yell that fucker's name. And as he swings around, I wind up just like Dad taught me, minor-leaguer, and when I release the charred remnants of my sister, and watch how perfectly the tiny fragments of her bones, the magnificent arc of her ashes, when I watch them spray all over Nick, in his eyes, up his nose, it's like in that very moment, I get what cheering was for Sabine.

And Connor, as Nick tries to shake the ashes out of his eyes, that former wrestling champion, my hero, he moves in with a Tongan death grip. Nick's jagged bottle pops out of his hand, and I catch Martha as she slumps down into a puddle of pink gown. And then, it's just Sabine I hear as the rain soaks us to the bone.

Atta girl, Midge.

twenty-eight

Sabine died so suddenly. Nobody saw it coming. And part of why Mom and Dad had to blame Connor, well I understand that now. As Dad told me after the police sorted everything out, and after Nick—who will be tried as an adult for narcotics distribution with intent to harm, as well as kidnapping—was safely locked up, "Worse than having a child die is living with the fact that you couldn't protect her. Blaming Connor made it easier, somehow."

When my parents found out the truth about Sabine, her pregnancy, the abuse from Nick and all of her mind games, it was hard on them, like they had this daughter with a secret life. Dr. Stern though, I have to say, he really helped with it all. The "I-statements," the sharing our anger and sadness. It's like we're different now—a small, less scattered family. Dad's calmer, Mom's less preoccupied. And me? I have the Volvo back. I got my license the week after school got out, and the first thing I did was take Nona to bingo at Holy Redeemer. "This car, it suits you, *Nipote*," she said as we crisscrossed North Portland. I slapped one of those EARTH bumper stickers where the ART part of the word is called out in red, I slapped it right over the *Trample the weak. Hurtle the dead.* I want to know that Nick's tagline is under mine. That, in the end, Nick was the weak one.

*   *   *

Tonight, there's a party for Connor. A going away bash that his parents are throwing him. Suddenly, the boy's a hero. But, he's still going to Bend. As he put it, "A summer away might be just what I need. I haven't seen my dad in a while, and, you know, he's all about the 12-step life now. Might do me good."

"Seems there's a bit of that going around," I offered.

Maybe that's the new rite of passage for middle age. Belief in a power greater than oneself and swearing off booze.

As for me, I'm just happy junior year is over. And, as it turns out, I'll be spending my eighteenth birthday in Florence, Italy. Mom's secret? It wasn't a lover after all. She'd been planning a surprise for me, going behind my back for letters of recommendation from Bowerman, McConnell, and even Lilith Cupworth. Things are not always what they seem. I'll be attending the Young Artists Summer Abroad Program, working with some of the best art teachers in the world, walking the same streets as the masters did, centuries ago.

And, as it turns out, I might see Martha on those same cobblestone streets. Rose Festival Queens travel, apparently, spreading the gospel of Portland, and all its wonders. Martha is now into yoga instead of Xanax, and she keeps telling me and Connor—and that scoop-seeking reporter, Rory Davis—that she owes us her life.

Heroics aside, I have a sketch to finish up at the Cupworth Studio. There's an element to the Connor sketch I need to add. An homage, I guess. Sort of like The Last Supper, where da Vinci wrote a story on his canvas. The last moment of grace before the fall. I need to put Sabine back on top. Her gorgeously arched form, the perfect balance, a foot cupped in her partner's hand. The moment before.

the end

Acknowledgements

To my writing group: Erin Leonard, Mary Wysong-Haeri, Diana Page Jordan, Monica Drake, Cheryl Strayed, Chuck Palahniuk, Lidia Yuknavitch and Chelsea Cain, thank you for your guidance, support and energy. Your big ideas. The way you've all modeled success and tenacity through these many years. Not to mention all those bottles of wine.

BH2014: Shanna Mahin, Averil Dean, Amy Gesenhues and Teri Carter. You guys, my new best friends, I can't even begin to gush on how fortunate I feel to have stumbled into your worlds. (Thanks, Betsy.)

Erin Reel, true friend and supporter, thank you for your belief in my writing from one millennium to the other.

Tom Spanbauer: the reason I keep writing.

Melissa Sarver, thank you, thank you, thank you for continuing to believe in this book.

Jennifer Bennett, Patty Kinney, Kayla Williams and all the wonderful writers I met at Antioch, Los Angeles—that MFA program changed my life.

Love to the LitReactor peeps, and the students there, too.

Mary Cummings and the gang at Diversion Books, visionaries and pioneers, you guys are really aliens from another planet, right? And I mean that in the best way possible.

Laura McCulloch, Kelly Ambrose, and David Millstone my forever friends and cheerleaders. Thanks for years and years of laughter and support.

Lisa Wish, Marshall Anderson, and Helen. I've thought of you often while writing this book.

Ellen Urbani Gass, thank you for your cheerleader insights.

Katie Soulé, thank you for all your continued support and vision. Brendan, Lindsay, Thamires: best extended family ever! Dakota, I can't wait until you're old enough to read this. Wait, yes I can, because I'll be ancient by then.

To my Buffalo family, Frank and Evelyn Vitello. All of the Walker clan. Nothing but love.

A special thought to the people who died too soon. Including Frankie Vitello, Lisa Walker, Candace Mulligan, and Jean Anderson.

To the hills of Portland, upon which I've always worked out my half-baked ideas.

Leona Kline, original wordsmith and Scrabble tutor, thanks for filling my childhood with words and ideas, and Gerry Freisinger, thanks for your fantastic sense of humor, encouraging love and inappropriate email jokes.

Kirk, you are my white-boarding, idea-fueling, best, bestest friend. Thanks for hanging in there, and thanks for all the tea and muffins and sustenance delivered to my desk, and especially thanks for putting up with my, you know, moods.

My kids: Sam, Maggie, Carson, I took out the *OOOOOOOO, dude, you've been served* per your astute edit. I love you three so much. You inspire me every waking hour.

Cheers.